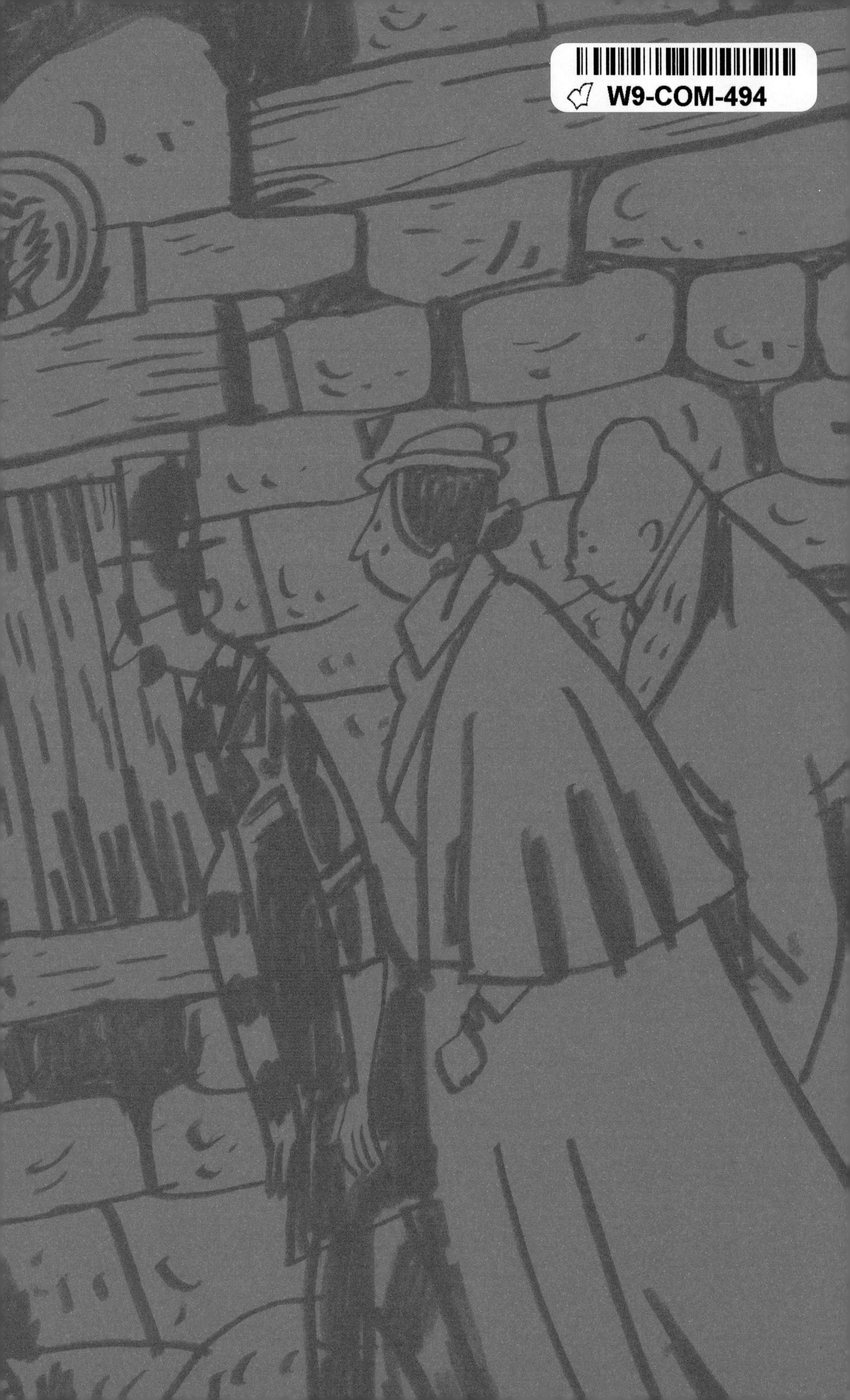

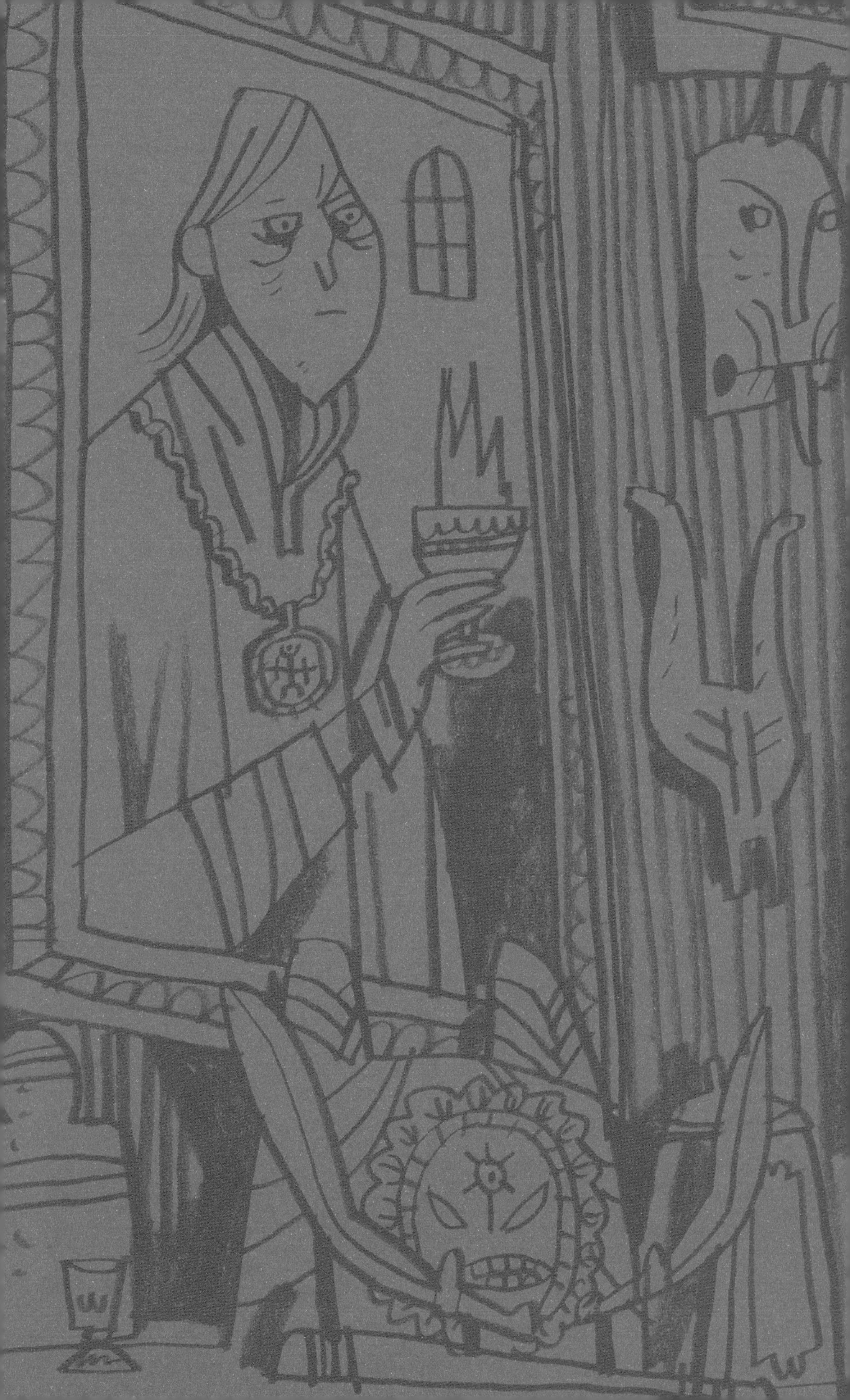

# FALCONSPEARE

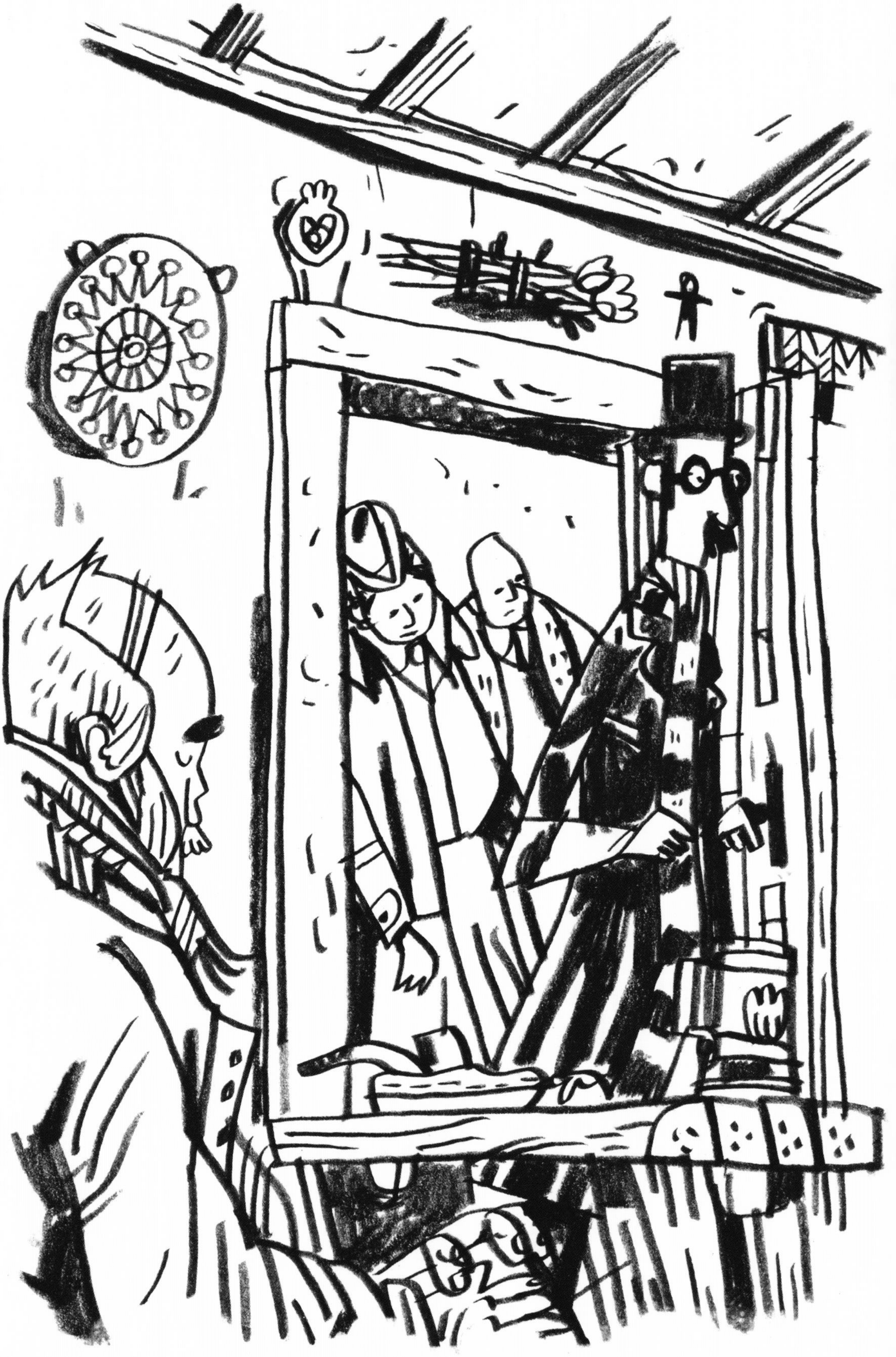

# FALCONSPEARE

Based on characters created by **MIKE MIGNOLA**
and **WARWICK JOHNSON-CADWELL**

*Story, Art, and Color by*
**WARWICK JOHNSON-CADWELL**

*Letters by*
**CLEM ROBINS**

*Cover by*
**MIKE MIGNOLA**
*with* **DAVE STEWART**

*President and Publisher* **MIKE RICHARDSON**
*Editor* **KATII O'BRIEN**
*Associate Editor* **JENNY BLENK**
*Collection Designer* **ETHAN KIMBERLING**
*Digital Art Technician* **ANN GRAY**

DARK HORSE BOOKS

Neil Hankerson *Executive Vice President* · Tom Weddle *Chief Financial Officer* · Dale LaFountain *Chief Information Officer* · Tim Wiesch *Vice President of Licensing* · Matt Parkinson *Vice President of Marketing* · Vanessa Todd-Holmes *Vice President of Production and Scheduling* · Mark Bernardi *Vice President of Book Trade and Digital Sales* · Ken Lizzi *General Counsel* · Dave Marshall *Editor in Chief* · Davey Estrada *Editorial Director* · Chris Warner *Senior Books Editor* · Cary Grazzini *Director of Specialty Projects* · Lia Ribacchi *Art Director* · Matt Dryer *Director of Digital Art and Prepress* · Michael Gombos *Senior Director of Licensed Publications* · Kari Yadro *Director of Custom Programs* · Kari Torson *Director of International Licensing* · Sean Brice *Director of Trade Sales* Randy Lahrman *Director of Product Sales*

Published by Dark Horse Books
A division of Dark Horse Comics LLC
10956 SE Main Street
Milwaukie, OR 97222

DarkHorse.com

Facebook.com/DarkHorseComics
Twitter.com/DarkHorseComics

First edition: December 2021
ebook ISBN 978-1-50672-477-5
ISBN 978-1-50672-476-8

1 3 5 7 9 10 8 6 4 2
Printed in China

*Library of Congress Cataloging-in-Publication Data*

*Names: Mignola, Mike, author. | Johnson-Cadwell, Warwick, author, artist. |*
  *Robins, Clem, 1955- letterer.*
*Title: Falconspeare / story by Mike Mignola and Warwick Johnson-Cadwell ;*
  *art and colors by Warwick Johnson-Cadwell ; letters by Clem Robins.*
*Description: First edition. | Milwaukie, OR : Dark Horse Books, 2021. |*
  *Summary: "Monster hunters extraordinaire Professor Meinhardt, Mr. Knox,*
  *and Ms. Van Sloan have teamed up to slay spooks and investigate the*
  *uncanny before, but now they'll tackle a question that's haunted them*
  *for years: What happened to their friend and vampire slayer*
  *extraordinaire, James Falconspeare?"-- Provided by publisher.*
*Identifiers: LCCN 2021008919 (print) | LCCN 2021008920 (ebook) | ISBN*
  *9781506724768 (hardcover) | ISBN 9781506724775 (ebook)*
*Subjects: LCSH: Graphic novels.*
*Classification: LCC PN6727.M53 F35 2021  (print) | LCC PN6727.M53  (ebook)*
  *| DDC 741.5/973--dc23*
*LC record available at https://lccn.loc.gov/2021008919*
*LC ebook record available at https://lccn.loc.gov/2021008920*

*This one is for my mum, who*
*I think liked this sort of thing.*
—WARWICK

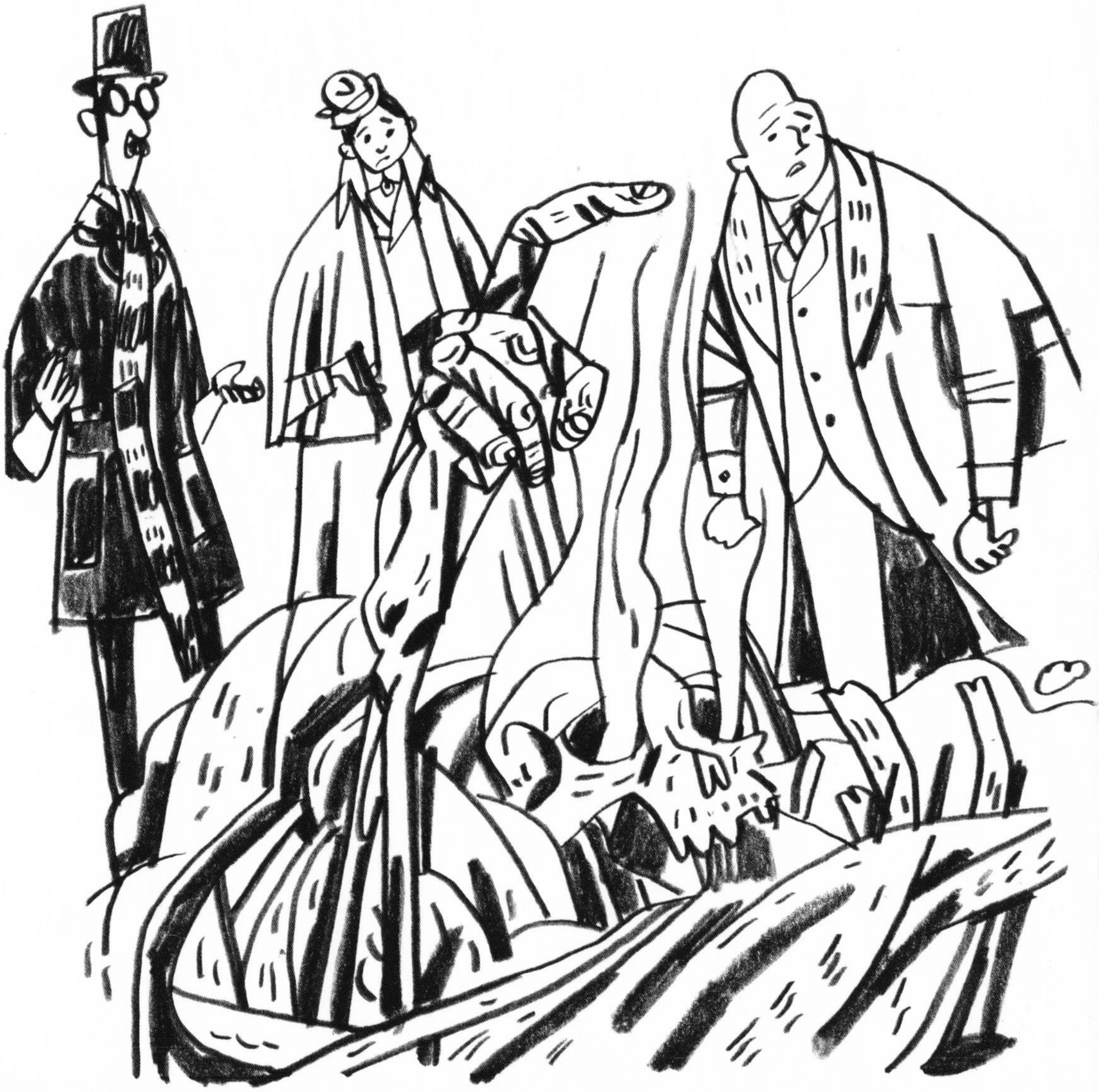

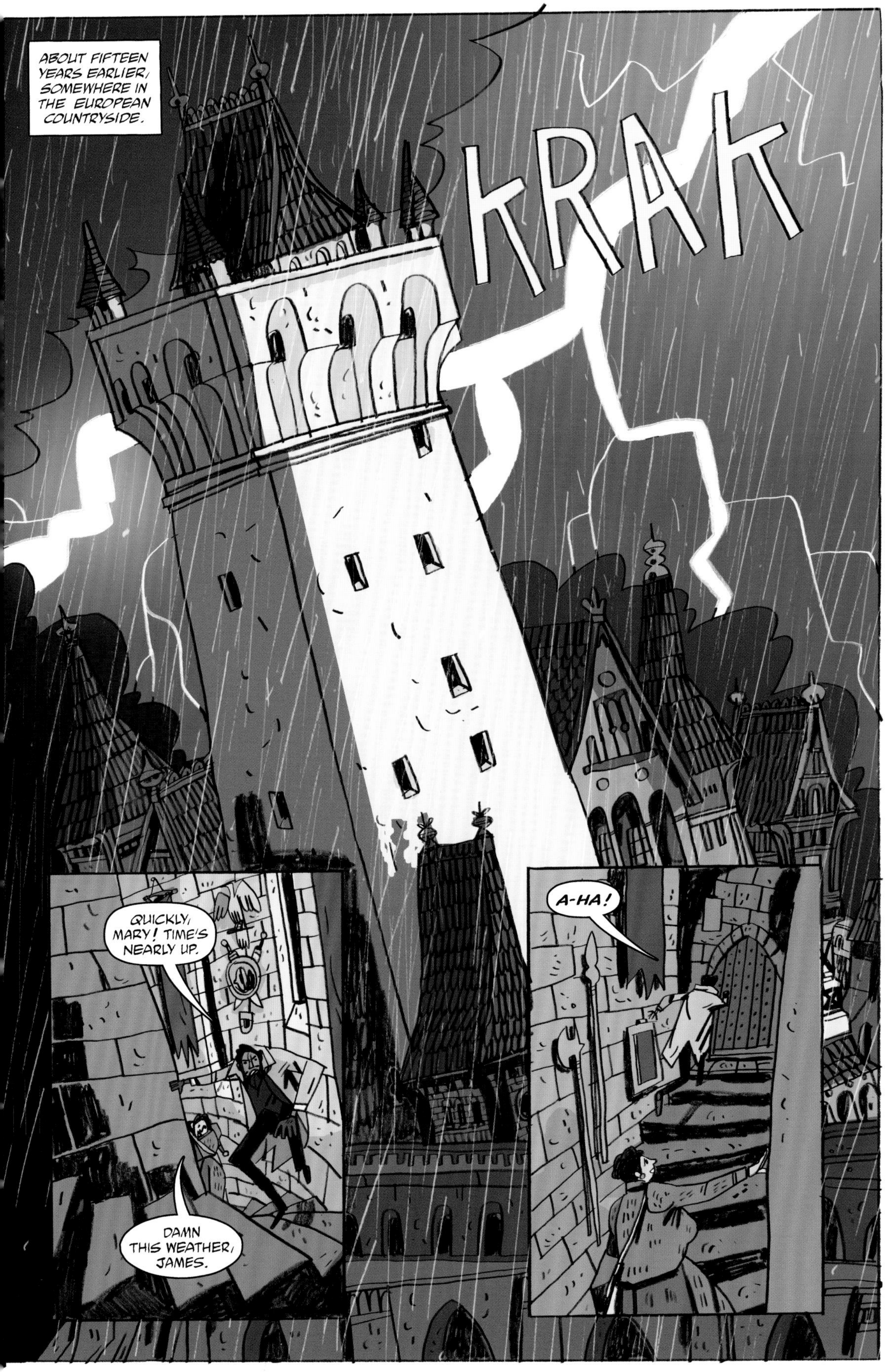
ABOUT FIFTEEN YEARS EARLIER, SOMEWHERE IN THE EUROPEAN COUNTRYSIDE.
KRAK
QUICKLY, MARY! TIME'S NEARLY UP.
DAMN THIS WEATHER, JAMES.
A-HA!

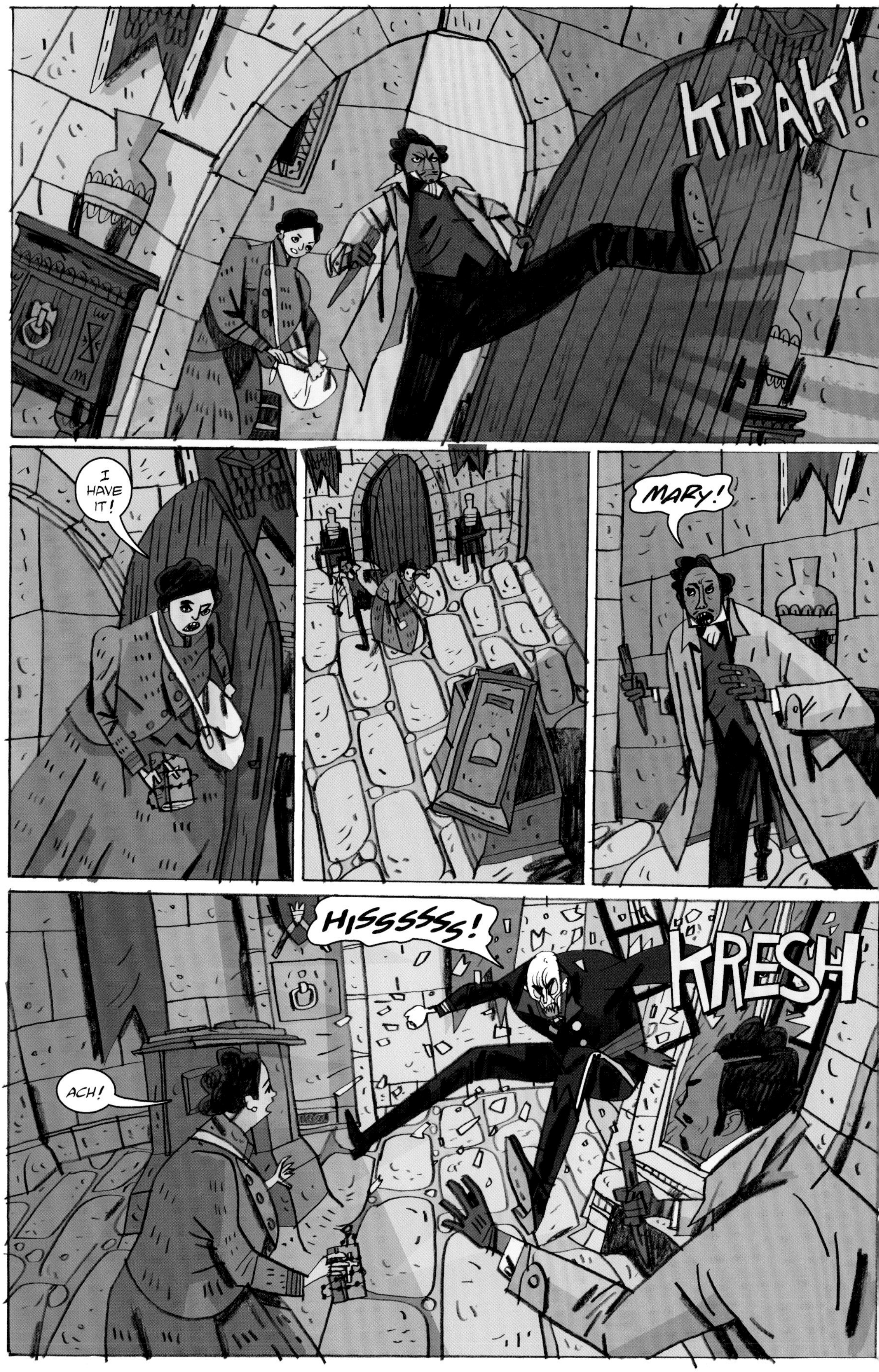
KRAK!
I HAVE IT!
MARY!
HISSSSSS!
KRESH
ACH!

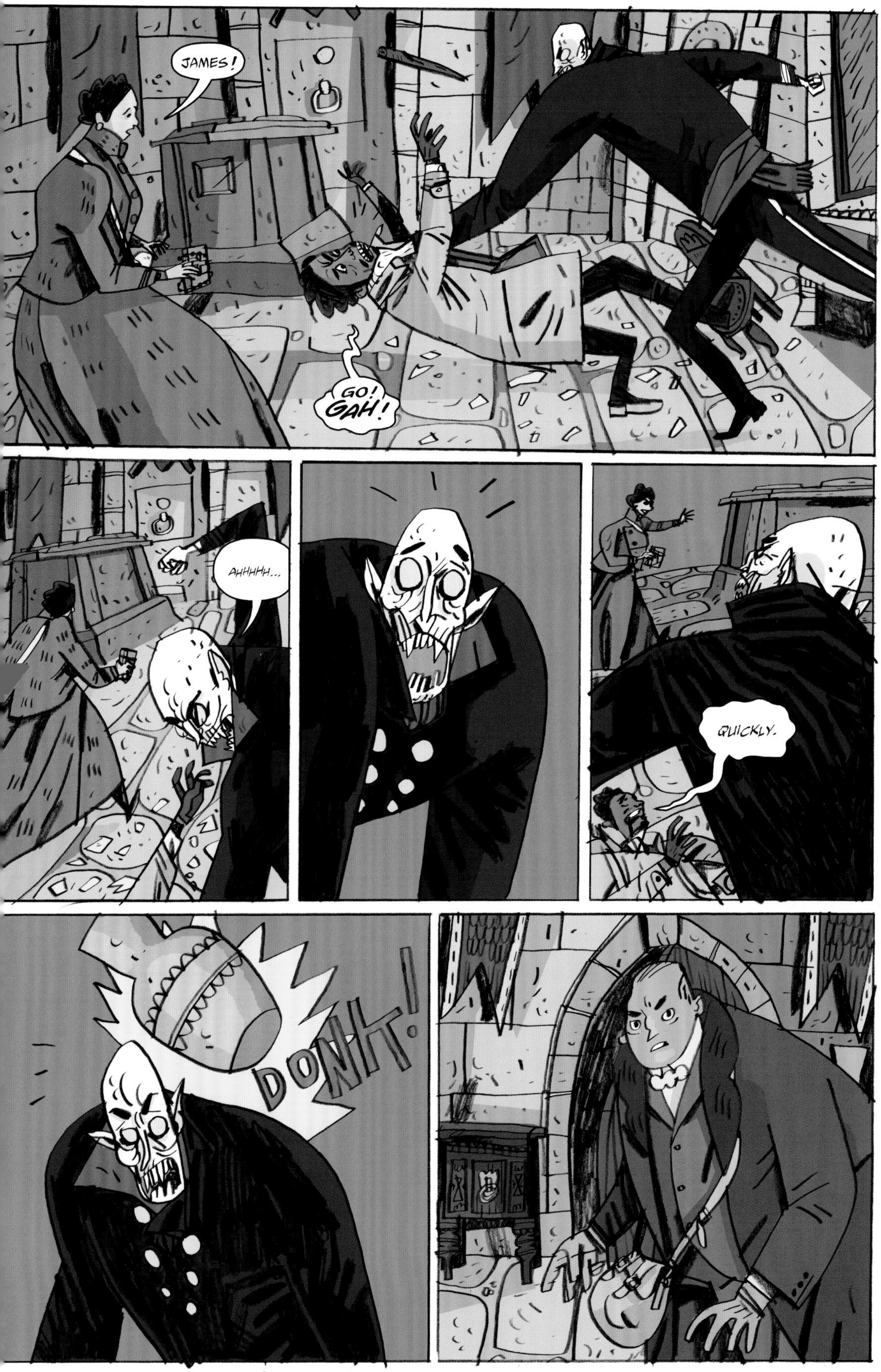
JAMES!
GO! GAH!
AHHHHH...
QUICKLY.
DONK!

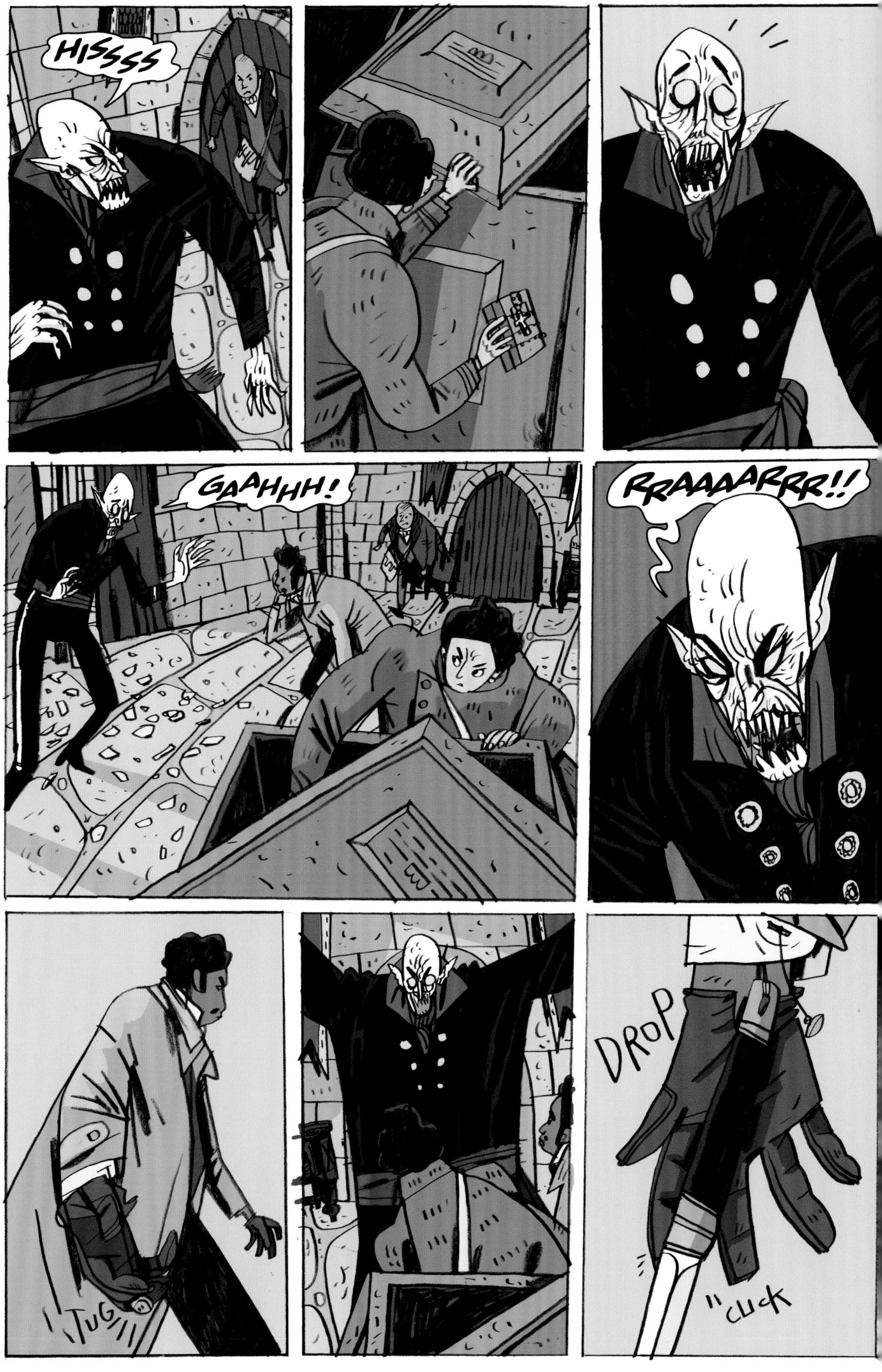
HISSSS
GAAHHH!
RRAAAAARRR!!
TUG
DROP
CLICK

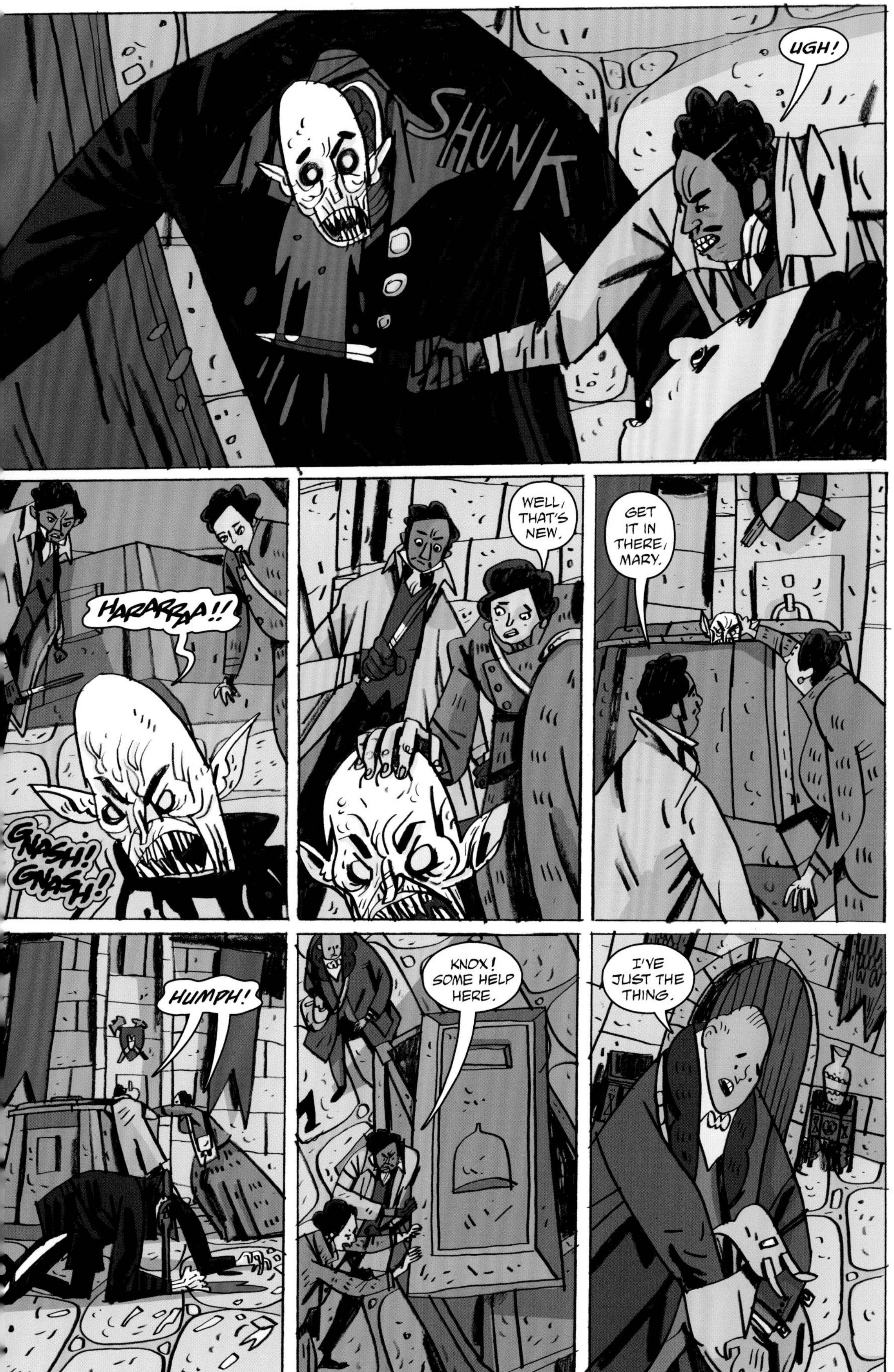
SHUNK
UGH!
HARARRA!!
GNASH! GNASH!
WELL, THAT'S NEW.
GET IT IN THERE, MARY.
HUMPH!
KNOX! SOME HELP HERE.
I'VE JUST THE THING.

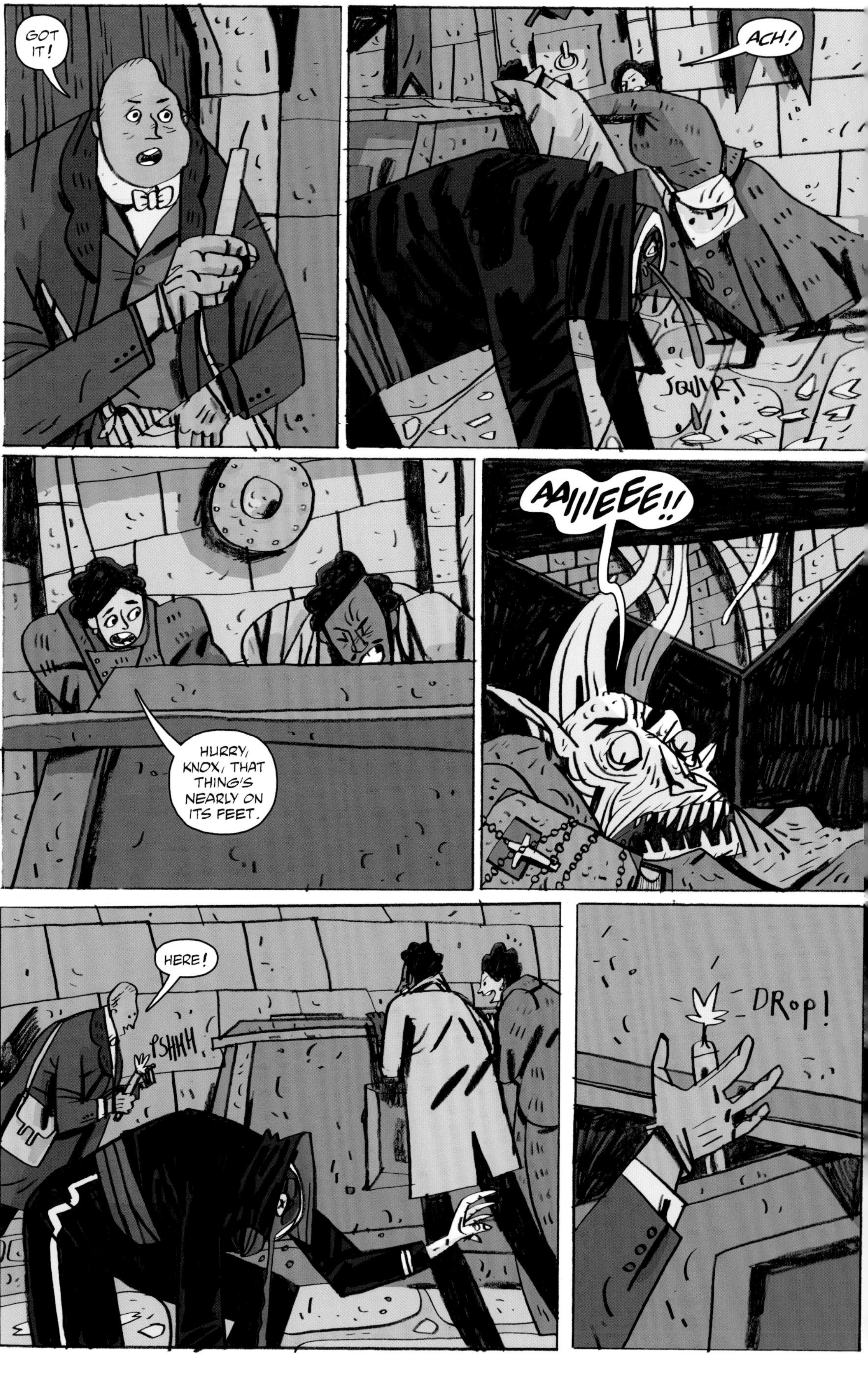
GOT IT!
ACH!
SQUIRT
HURRY, KNOX, THAT THING'S NEARLY ON ITS FEET.
AAIIIEEE!!
HERE!
PSHHH
DROP!

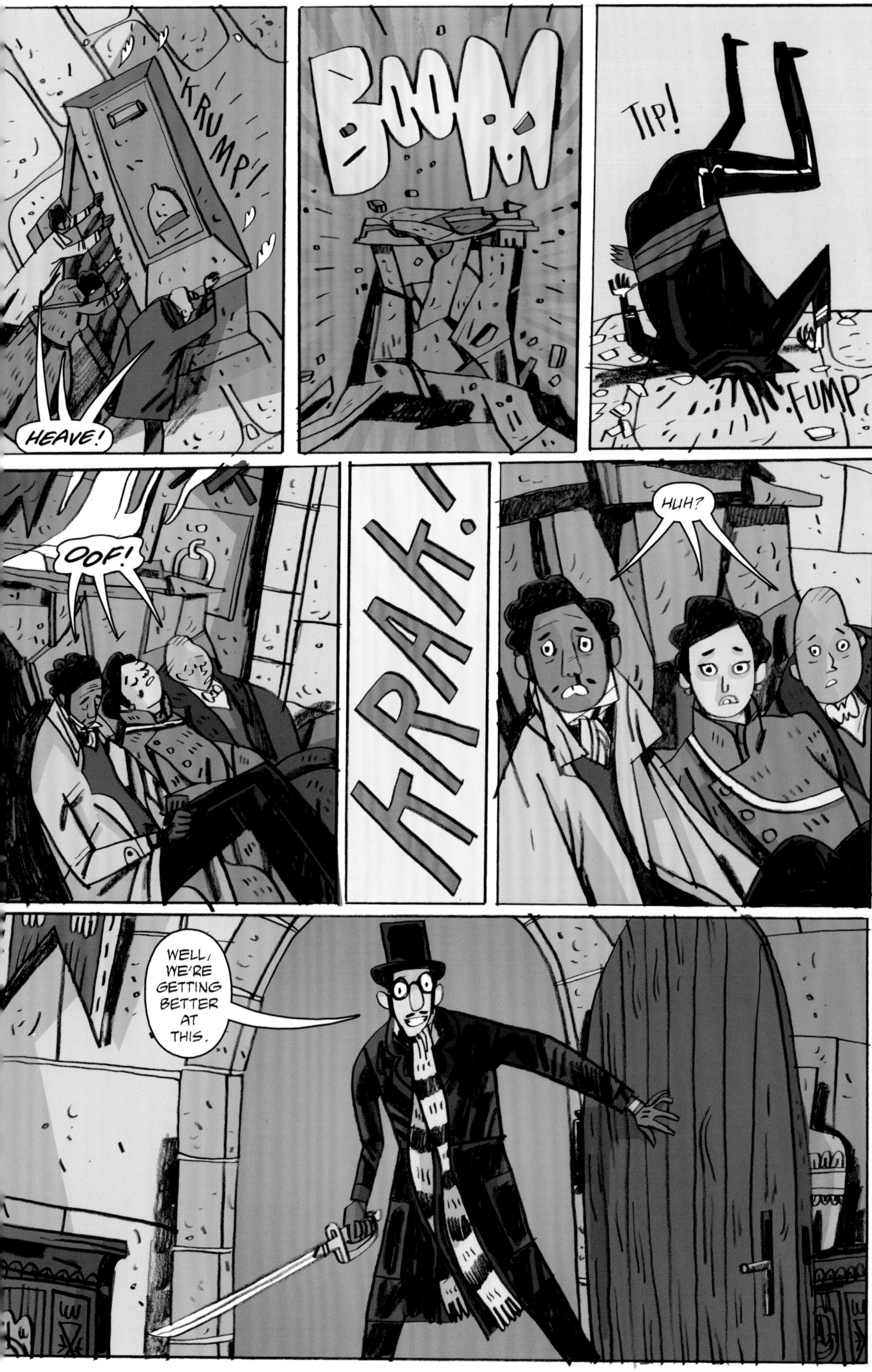
KRUMP!
HEAVE!
BOOM
TIP!
FUMP
OOF!
KRAK!
HUH?
WELL, WE'RE GETTING BETTER AT THIS.

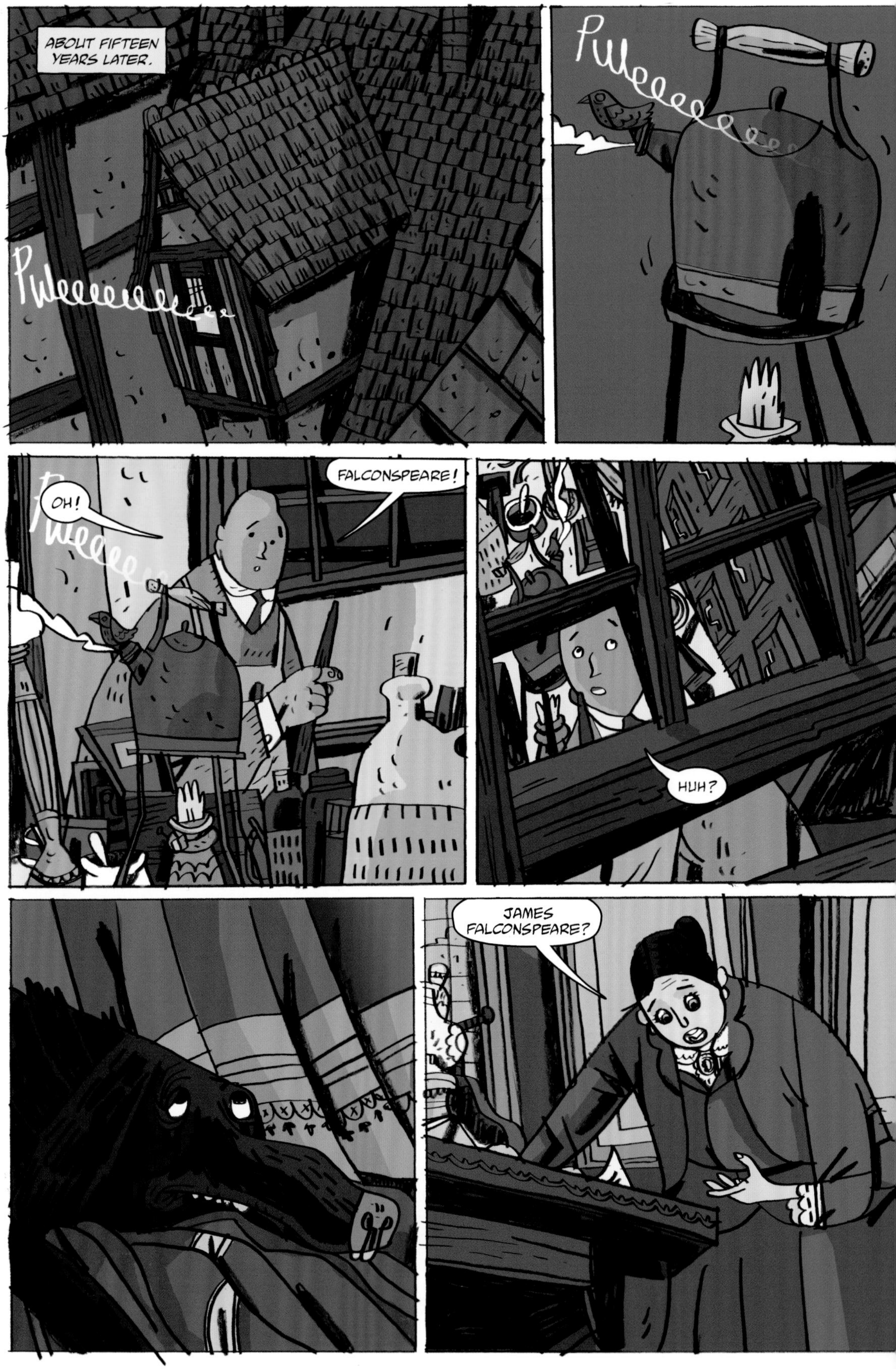

ABOUT FIFTEEN YEARS LATER.
Pwheeeeeeeeeee
Pwheeeeeeeeee
Pweeeeee
OH!
FALCONSPEARE!
HUH?
JAMES FALCONSPEARE?

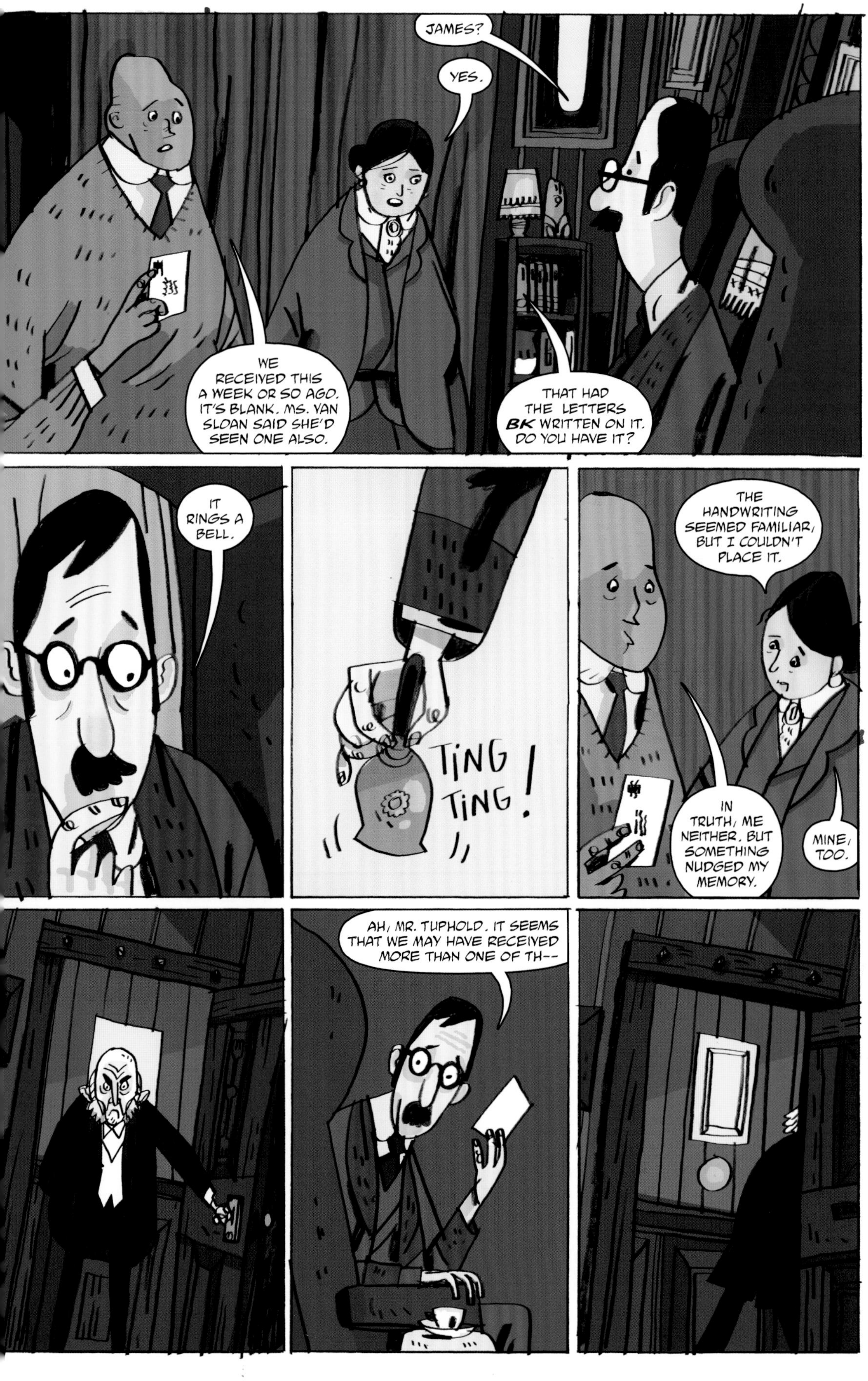
JAMES?
YES.
WE RECEIVED THIS A WEEK OR SO AGO. IT'S BLANK. MS. VAN SLOAN SAID SHE'D SEEN ONE ALSO.
THAT HAD THE LETTERS **BK** WRITTEN ON IT. DO YOU HAVE IT?
IT RINGS A BELL.
TING TING!
THE HANDWRITING SEEMED FAMILIAR, BUT I COULDN'T PLACE IT.
IN TRUTH, ME NEITHER. BUT SOMETHING NUDGED MY MEMORY.
MINE, TOO.
AH, MR. TUPHOLD. IT SEEMS THAT WE MAY HAVE RECEIVED MORE THAN ONE OF TH--

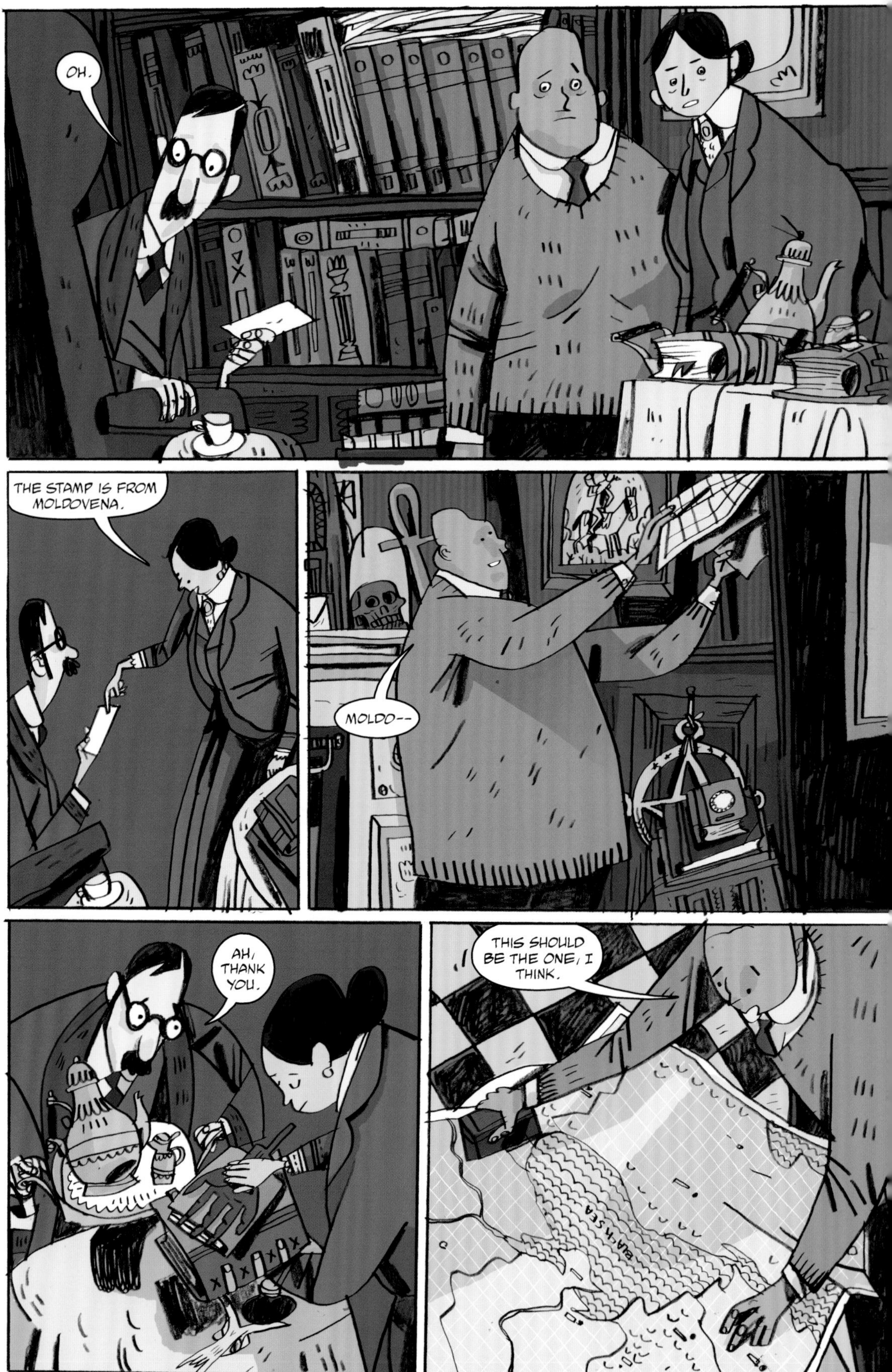
OH.
THE STAMP IS FROM MOLDOVENA.
MOLDO--
AH, THANK YOU.
THIS SHOULD BE THE ONE, I THINK.

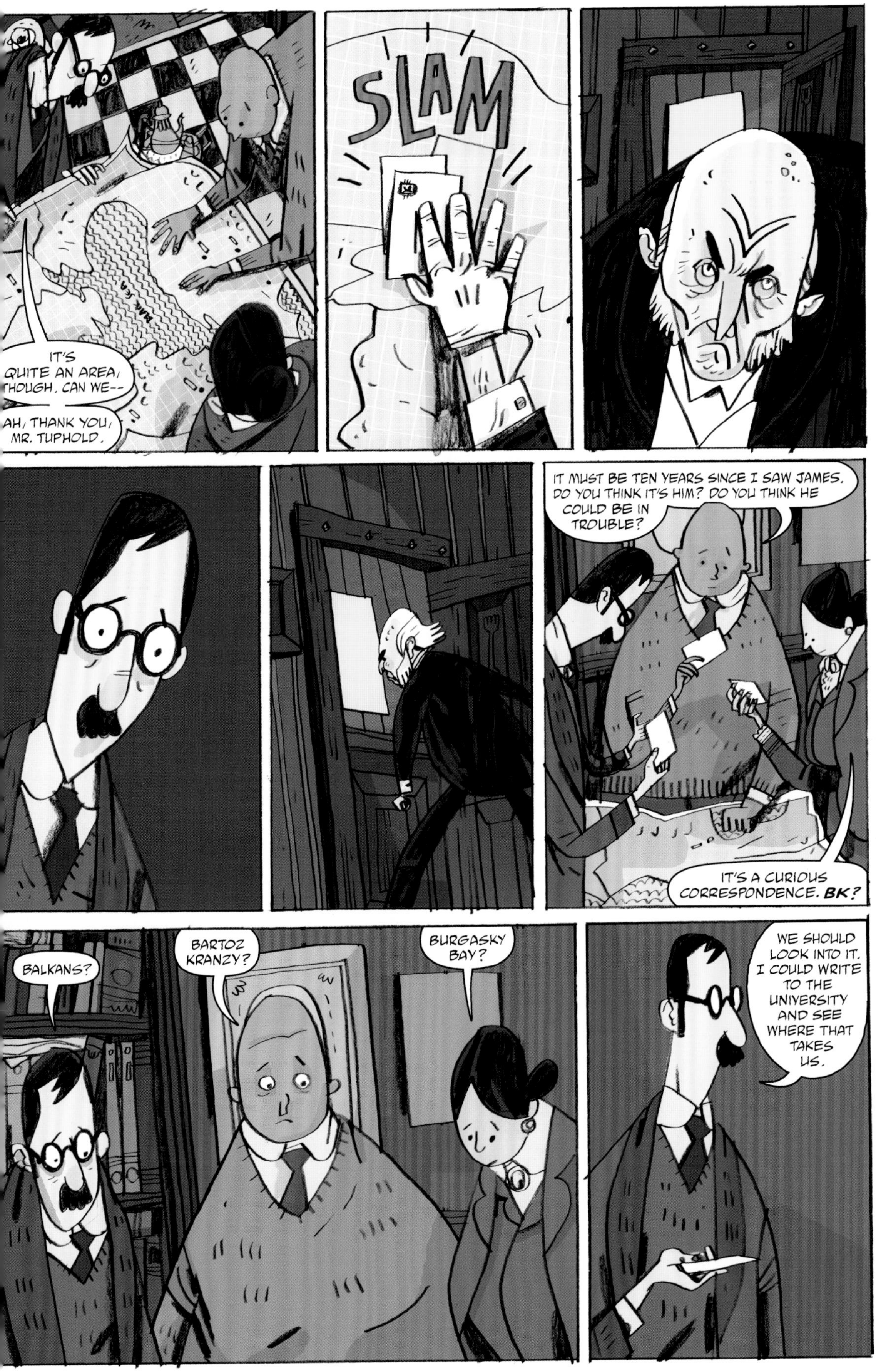
IT'S QUITE AN AREA, THOUGH. CAN WE--
AH, THANK YOU, MR. TUPHOLD.
SLAM
IT MUST BE TEN YEARS SINCE I SAW JAMES. DO YOU THINK IT'S HIM? DO YOU THINK HE COULD BE IN TROUBLE?
IT'S A CURIOUS CORRESPONDENCE. BK?
BALKANS?
BARTOZ KRANZY?
BURGASKY BAY?
WE SHOULD LOOK INTO IT. I COULD WRITE TO THE UNIVERSITY AND SEE WHERE THAT TAKES US.

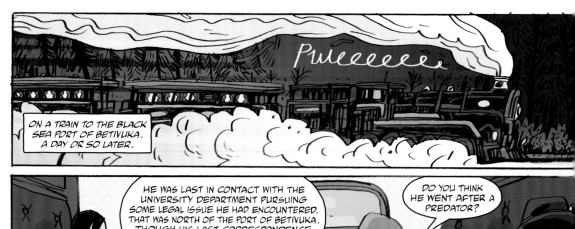

ON A TRAIN TO THE BLACK SEA PORT OF BETIVUKA, A DAY OR SO LATER.

HE WAS LAST IN CONTACT WITH THE UNIVERSITY DEPARTMENT PURSUING SOME LEGAL ISSUE HE HAD ENCOUNTERED. THAT WAS NORTH OF THE PORT OF BETIVUKA, THOUGH HIS LAST CORRESPONDENCE WITH THEM SUGGESTED HE WAS MAKING HIS WAY TO THE BLACK DOCKS THERE.

DO YOU THINK HE WENT AFTER A PREDATOR?

NOT **CERTAIN** AT ALL, BUT...

THEY'VE HAD AN ONGOING ISSUE WITH THIS ASSAILANT, **"THE BITER."** LOCAL REPORTS ARGUE THAT THESE MAY BE VAMPIRE ATTACKS, AND I CAN TRUST THAT JAMES MAY HAVE DECIDED TO TACKLE THEM.

SINCE THAT LAST CORRESPONDENCE WITH THE UNIVERSITY, THEY'VE HAD NO WORD OF HIM.

MY CURIOSITY HAS GROWN INTO CONCERN.

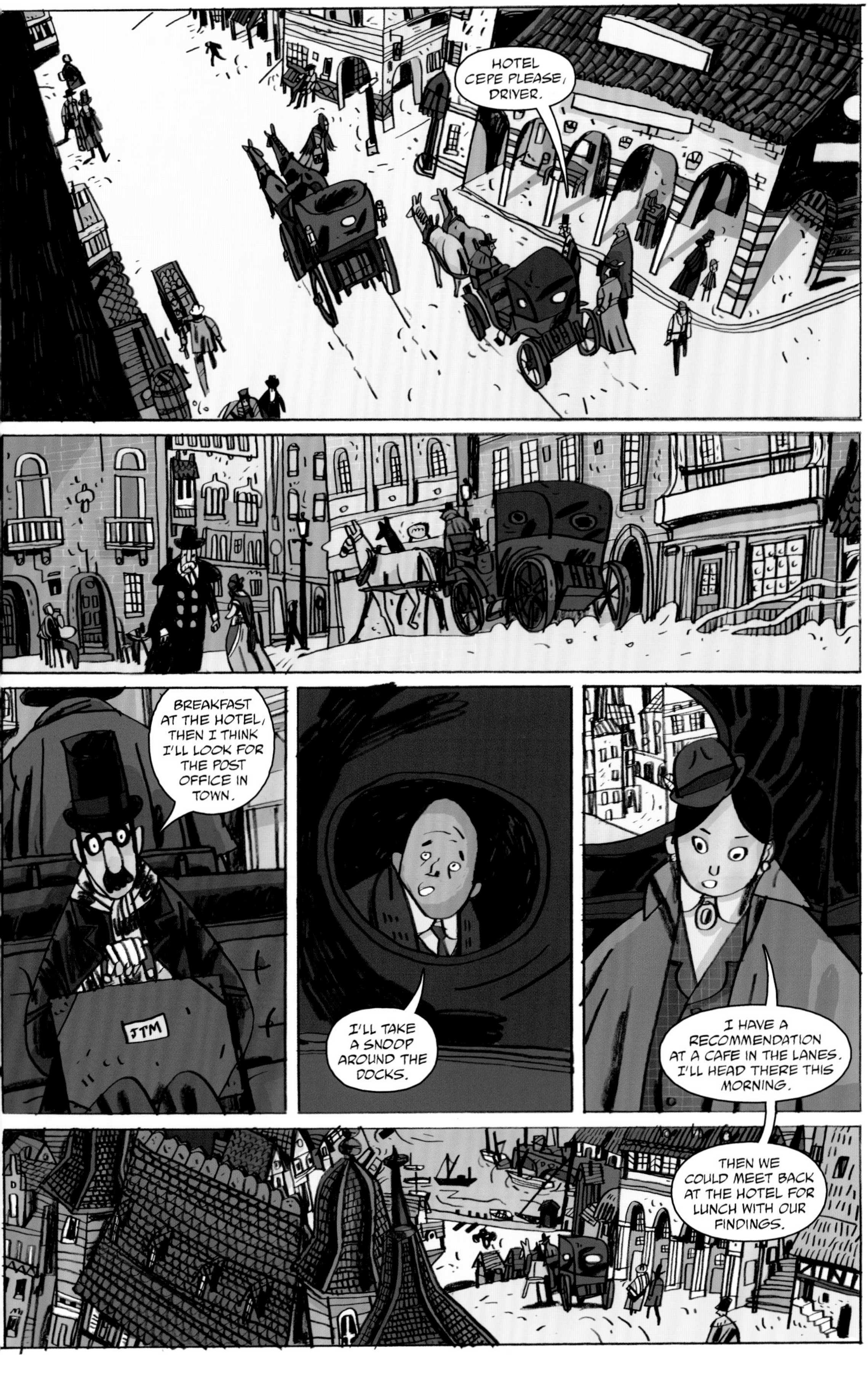
HOTEL CEPE PLEASE, DRIVER.
BREAKFAST AT THE HOTEL, THEN I THINK I'LL LOOK FOR THE POST OFFICE IN TOWN.
JTM
I'LL TAKE A SNOOP AROUND THE DOCKS.
I HAVE A RECOMMENDATION AT A CAFE IN THE LANES. I'LL HEAD THERE THIS MORNING.
THEN WE COULD MEET BACK AT THE HOTEL FOR LUNCH WITH OUR FINDINGS.

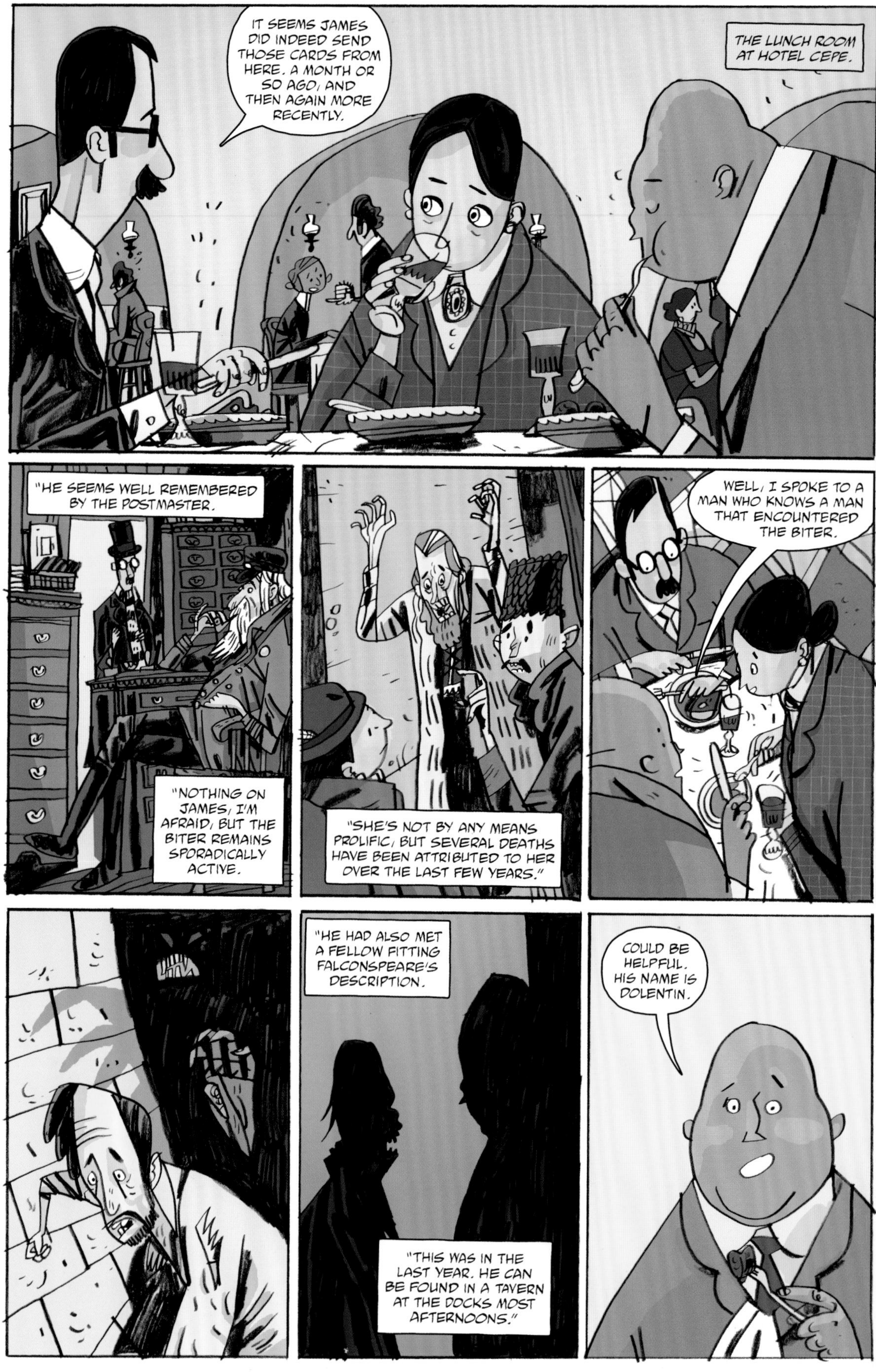

THE LUNCH ROOM AT HOTEL CEPE.
IT SEEMS JAMES DID INDEED SEND THOSE CARDS FROM HERE. A MONTH OR SO AGO, AND THEN AGAIN MORE RECENTLY.
"HE SEEMS WELL REMEMBERED BY THE POSTMASTER.
"NOTHING ON JAMES, I'M AFRAID, BUT THE BITER REMAINS SPORADICALLY ACTIVE.
"SHE'S NOT BY ANY MEANS PROLIFIC, BUT SEVERAL DEATHS HAVE BEEN ATTRIBUTED TO HER OVER THE LAST FEW YEARS."
WELL, I SPOKE TO A MAN WHO KNOWS A MAN THAT ENCOUNTERED THE BITER.
"HE HAD ALSO MET A FELLOW FITTING FALCONSPEARE'S DESCRIPTION.
"THIS WAS IN THE LAST YEAR. HE CAN BE FOUND IN A TAVERN AT THE DOCKS MOST AFTERNOONS."
COULD BE HELPFUL. HIS NAME IS DOLENTIN.

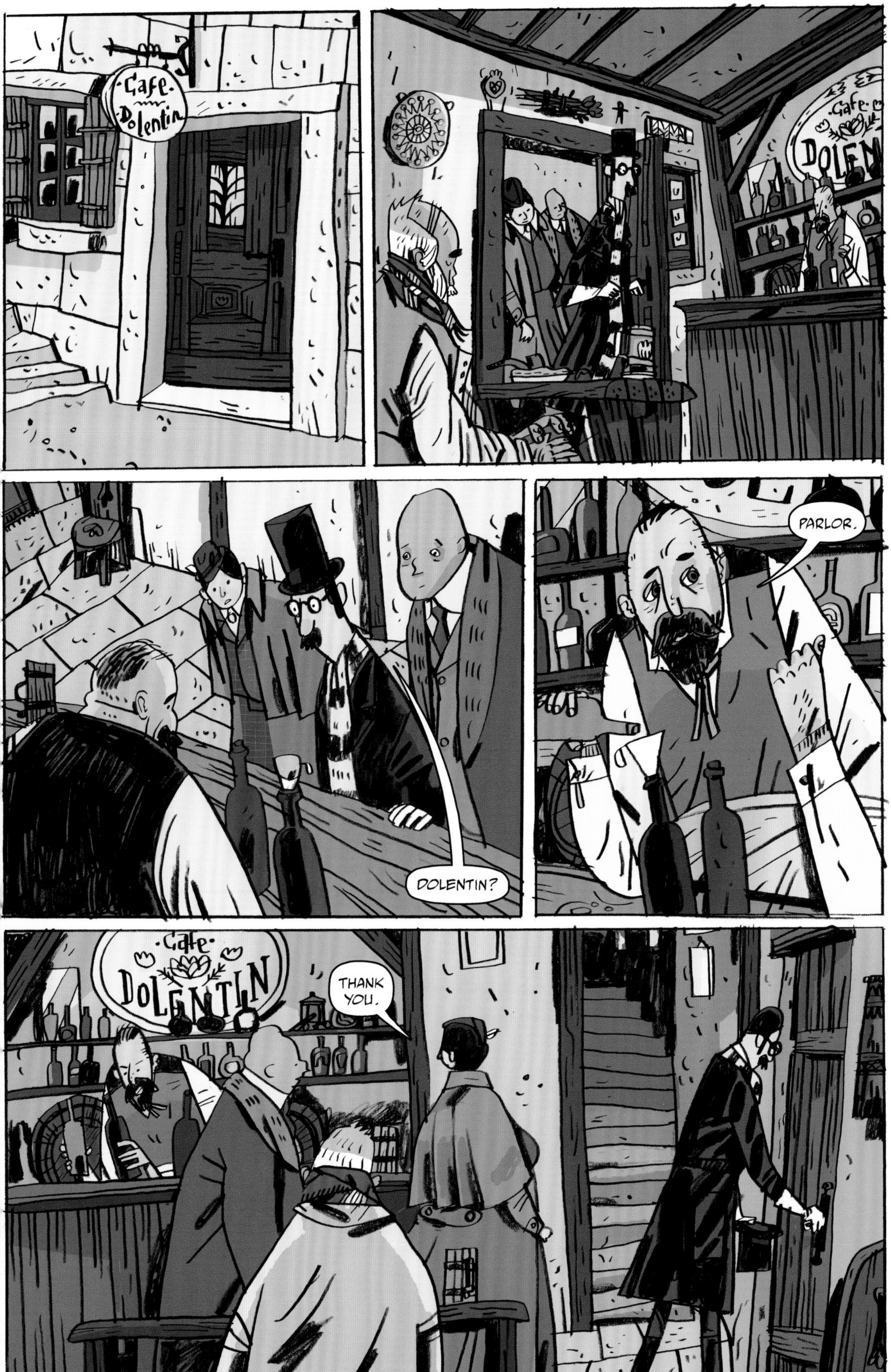

Cafe Dolentin
Cafe Dolentin
DOLENTIN?
PARLOR.
Cafe DOLENTIN
THANK YOU.

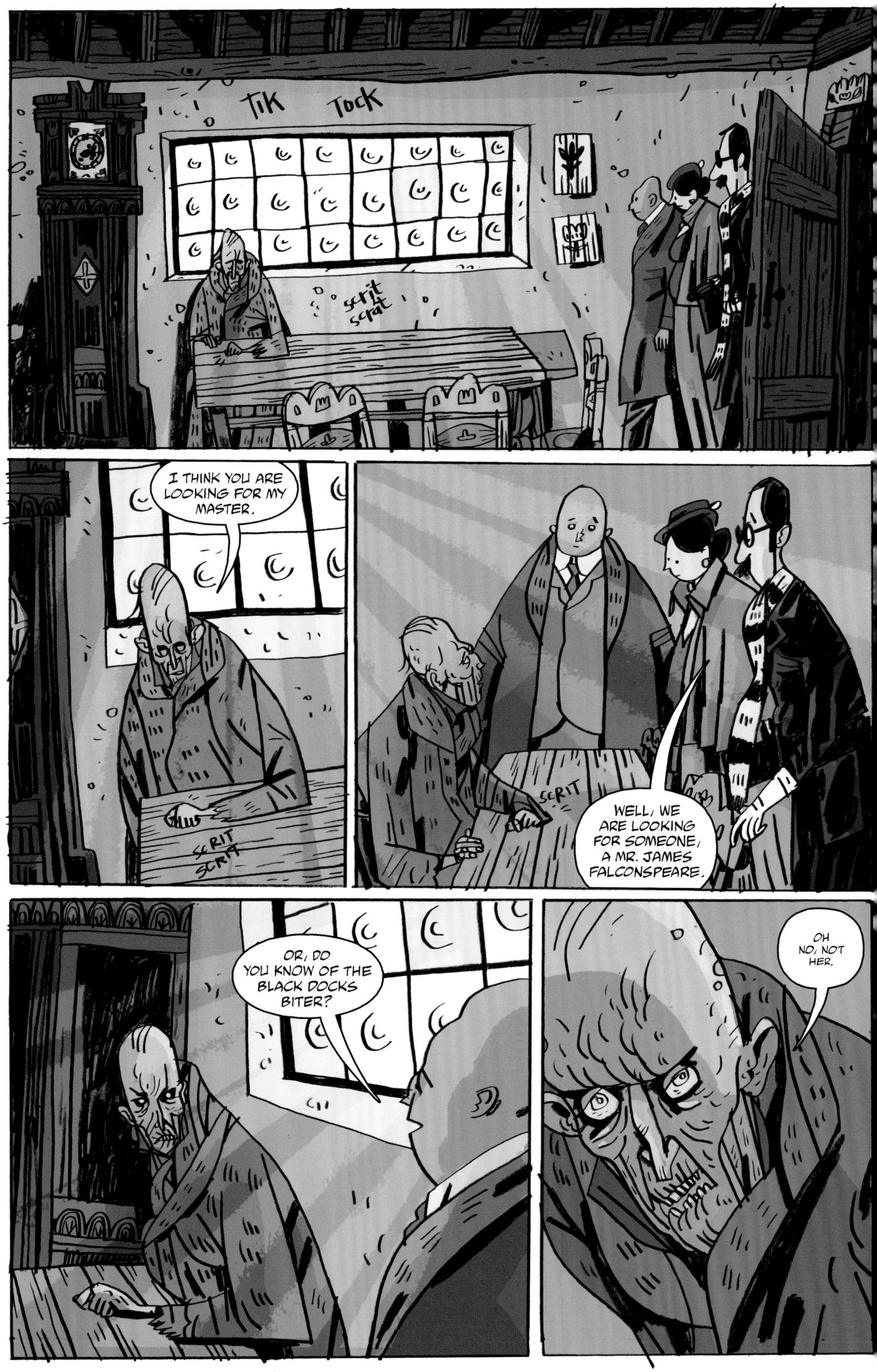
TIK
TOCK
SCRIT SCRAT
I THINK YOU ARE LOOKING FOR MY MASTER.
SCRIT SCRIT
SCRIT
WELL, WE ARE LOOKING FOR SOMEONE, A MR. JAMES FALCONSPEARE.
OR, DO YOU KNOW OF THE BLACK DOCKS BITER?
OH NO, NOT HER.

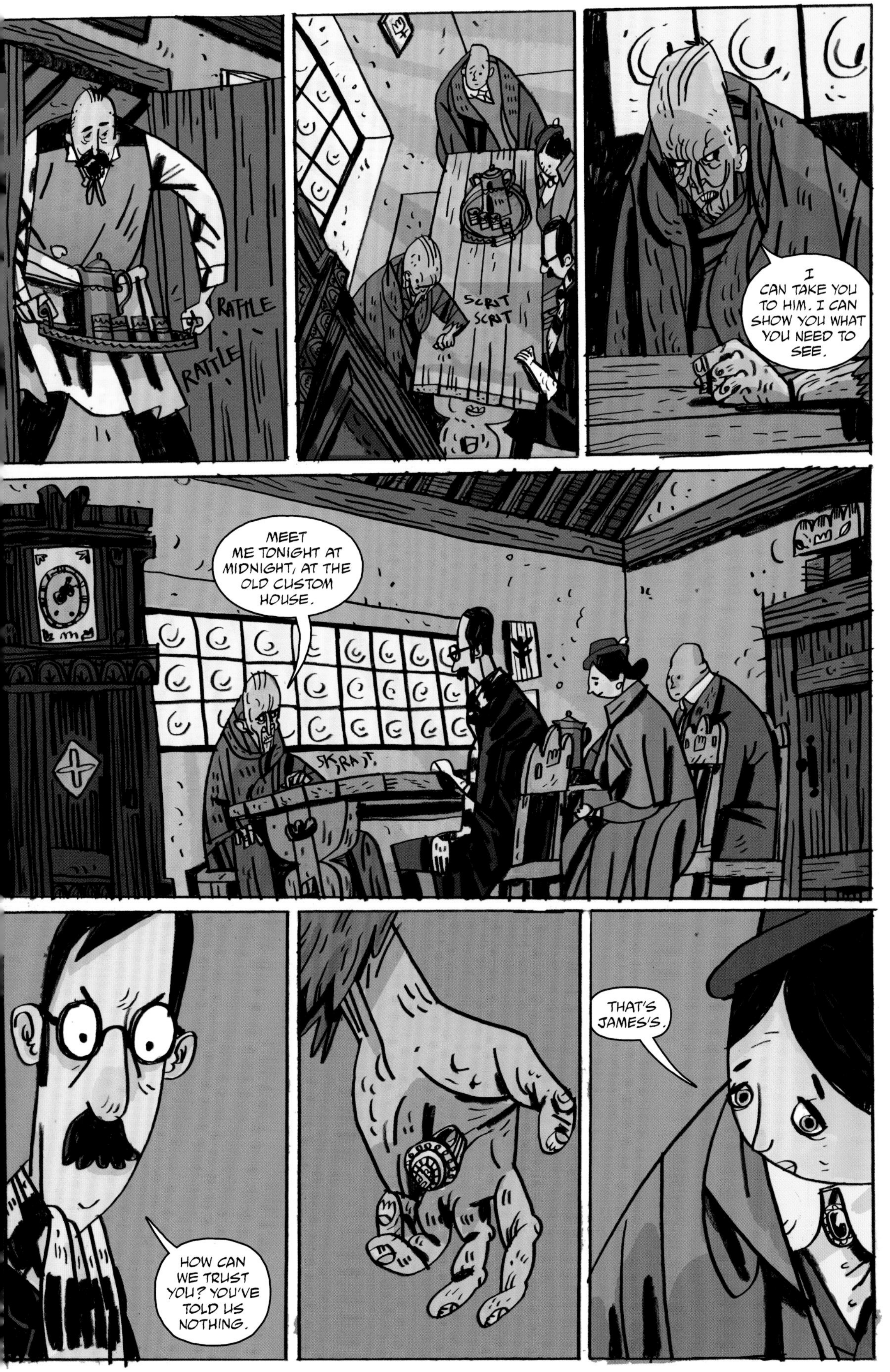
RATTLE
RATTLE
SCRIT
SCRIT
I CAN TAKE YOU TO HIM. I CAN SHOW YOU WHAT YOU NEED TO SEE.
MEET ME TONIGHT AT MIDNIGHT, AT THE OLD CUSTOM HOUSE.
SKRAT
HOW CAN WE TRUST YOU? YOU'VE TOLD US NOTHING.
THAT'S JAMES'S.

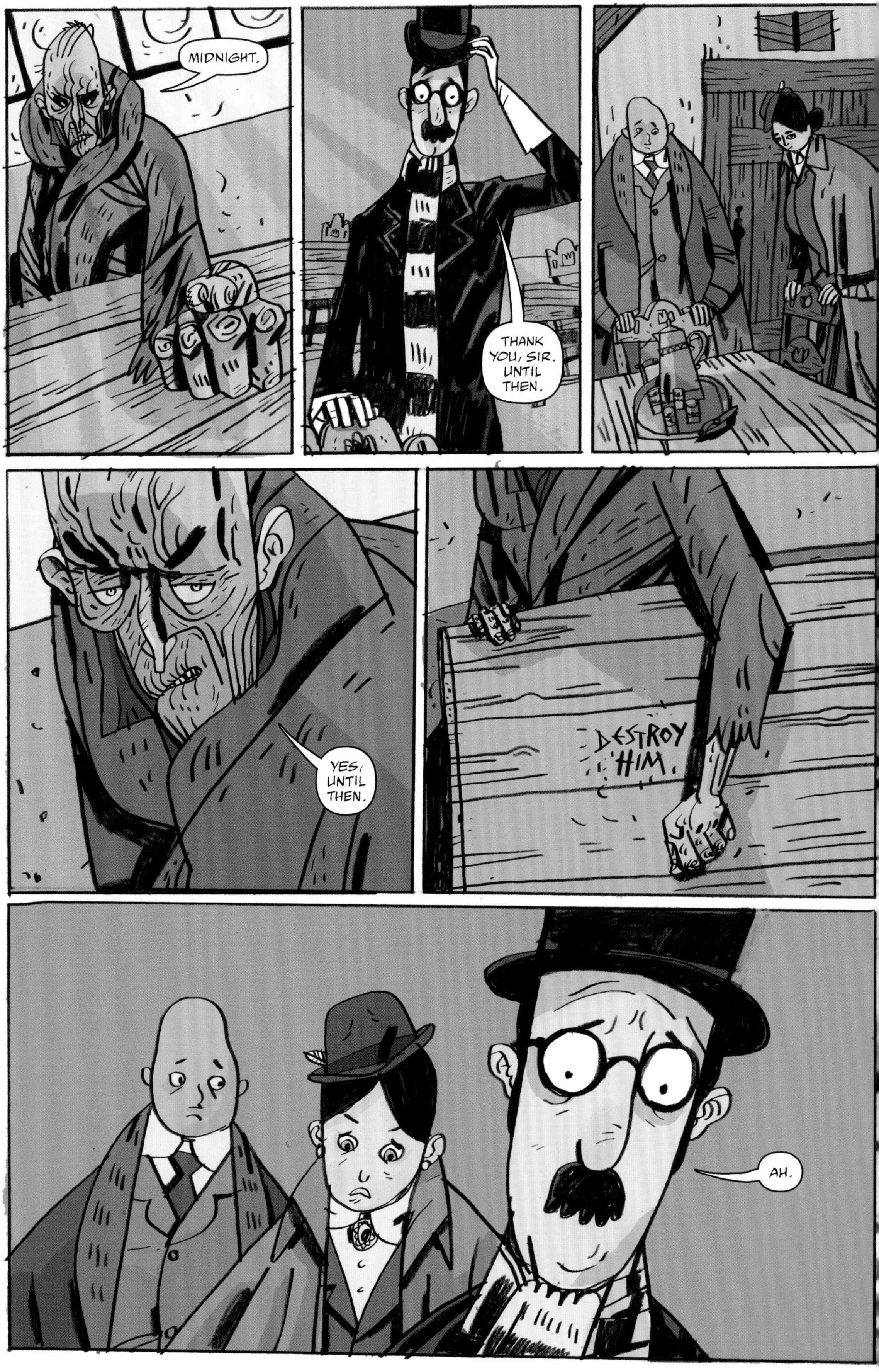
MIDNIGHT.
THANK YOU, SIR. UNTIL THEN.
YES, UNTIL THEN.
DESTROY HIM
AH.

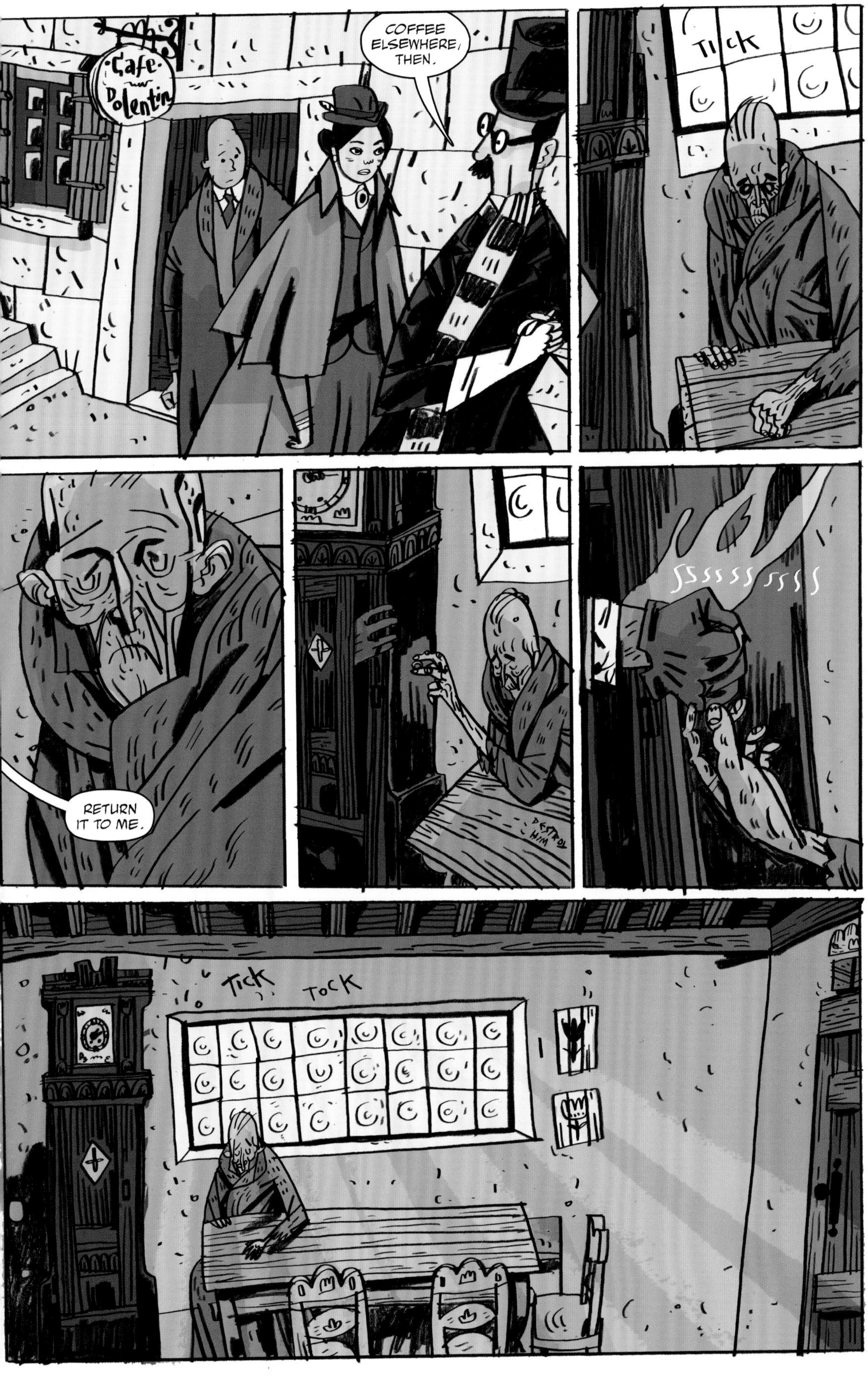
Cafe Dolentin
COFFEE ELSEWHERE, THEN.
TICK
RETURN IT TO ME.
DESTROY HIM
SSSSSSSSSS
TICK
TOCK

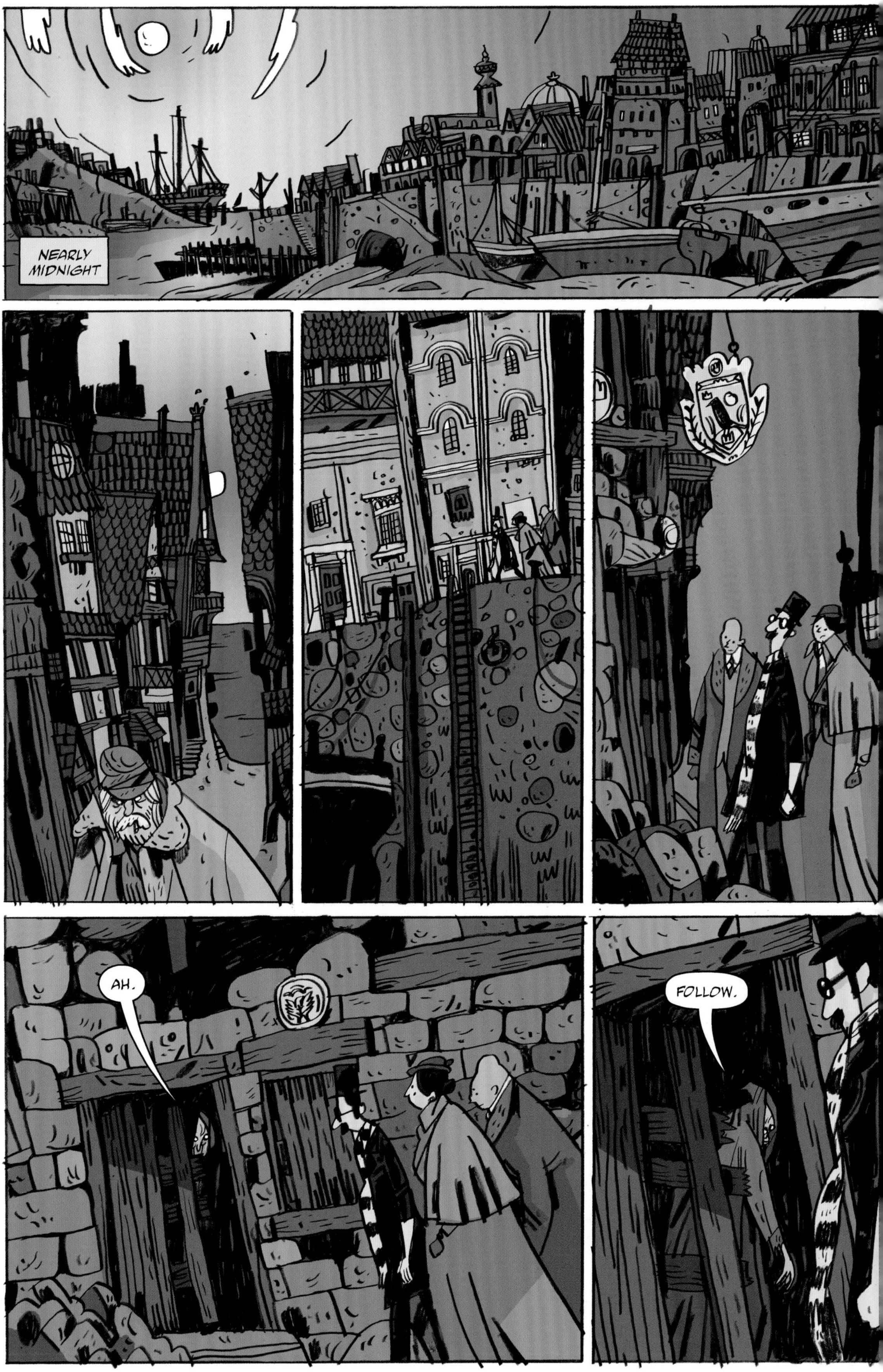
NEARLY MIDNIGHT
AH.
FOLLOW.

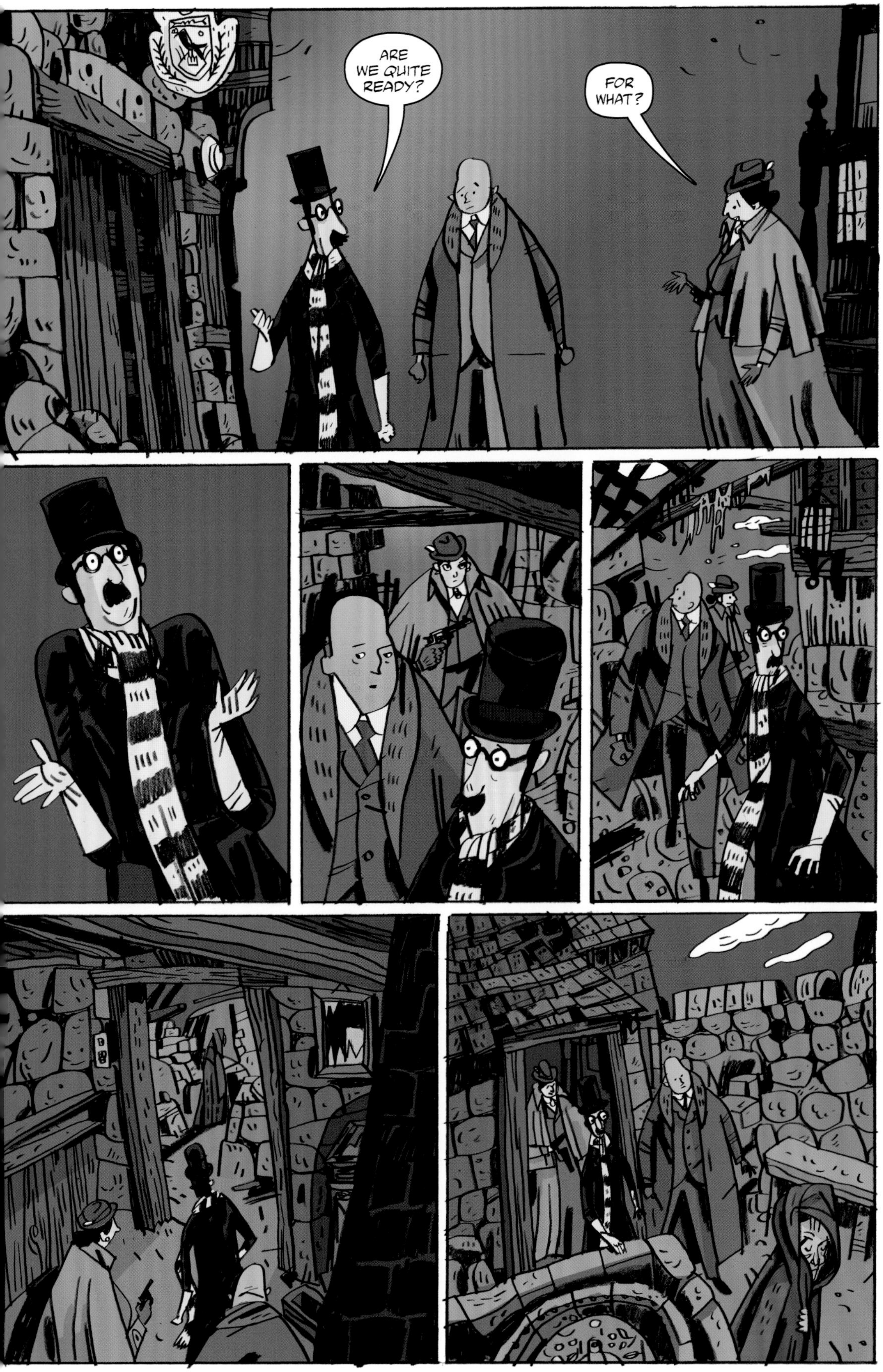
ARE WE QUITE READY?
FOR WHAT?

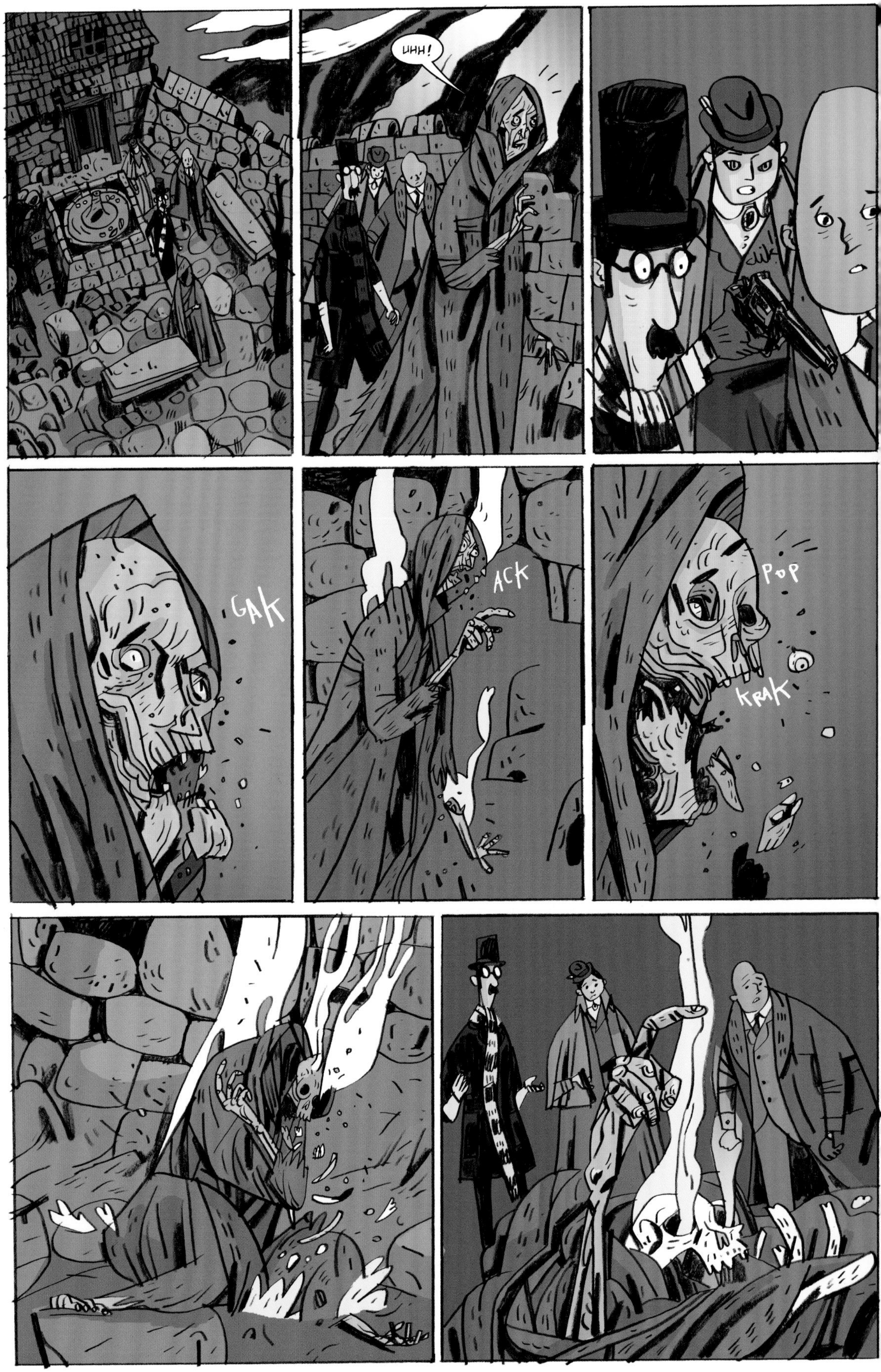
UHH!
GAK
ACK
POP
KRAK

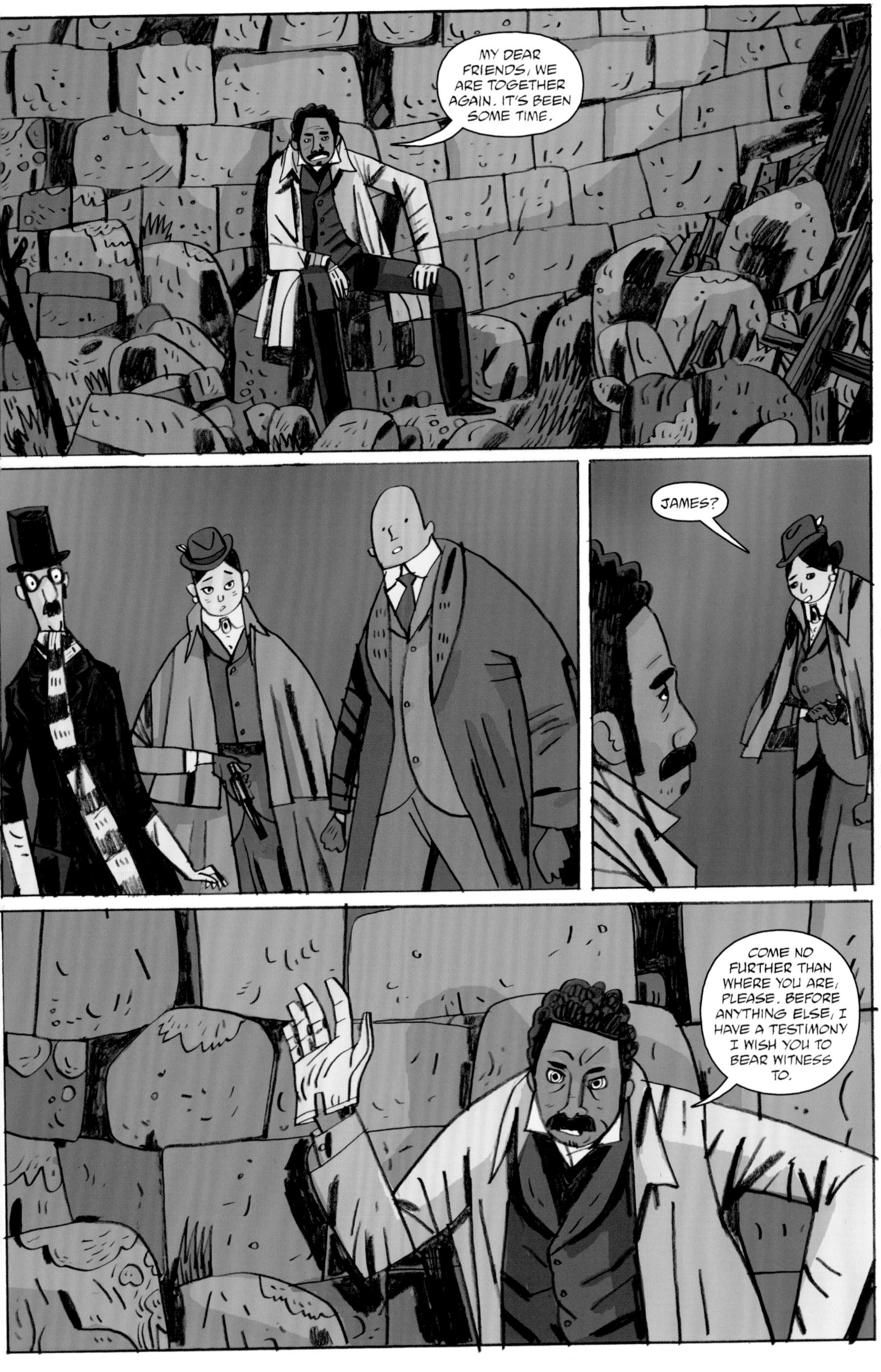
MY DEAR FRIENDS, WE ARE TOGETHER AGAIN. IT'S BEEN SOME TIME.
JAMES?
COME NO FURTHER THAN WHERE YOU ARE, PLEASE. BEFORE ANYTHING ELSE, I HAVE A TESTIMONY I WISH YOU TO BEAR WITNESS TO.

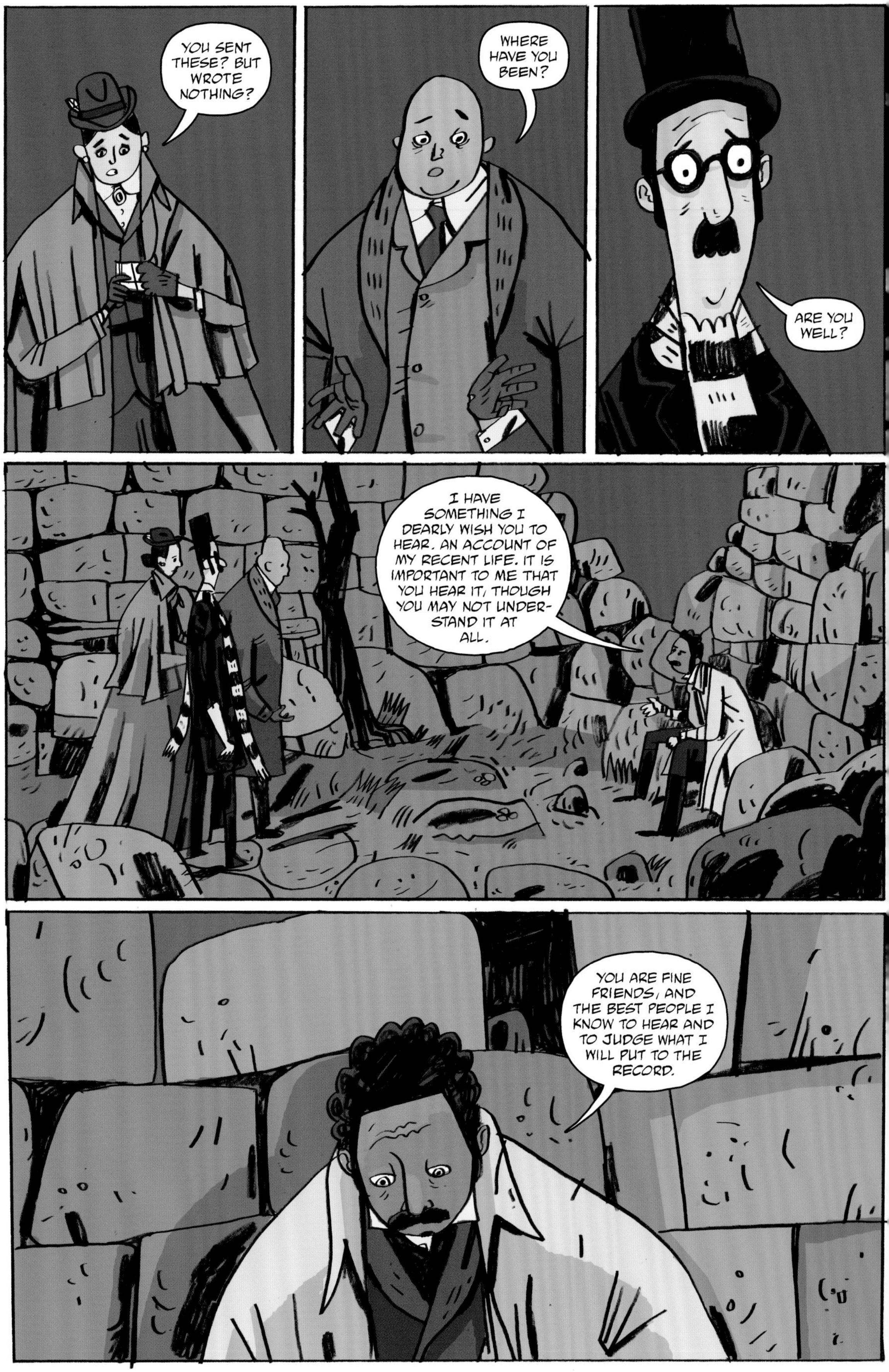
YOU SENT THESE? BUT WROTE NOTHING?
WHERE HAVE YOU BEEN?
ARE YOU WELL?
I HAVE SOMETHING I DEARLY WISH YOU TO HEAR. AN ACCOUNT OF MY RECENT LIFE. IT IS IMPORTANT TO ME THAT YOU HEAR IT, THOUGH YOU MAY NOT UNDERSTAND IT AT ALL.
YOU ARE FINE FRIENDS, AND THE BEST PEOPLE I KNOW TO HEAR AND TO JUDGE WHAT I WILL PUT TO THE RECORD.

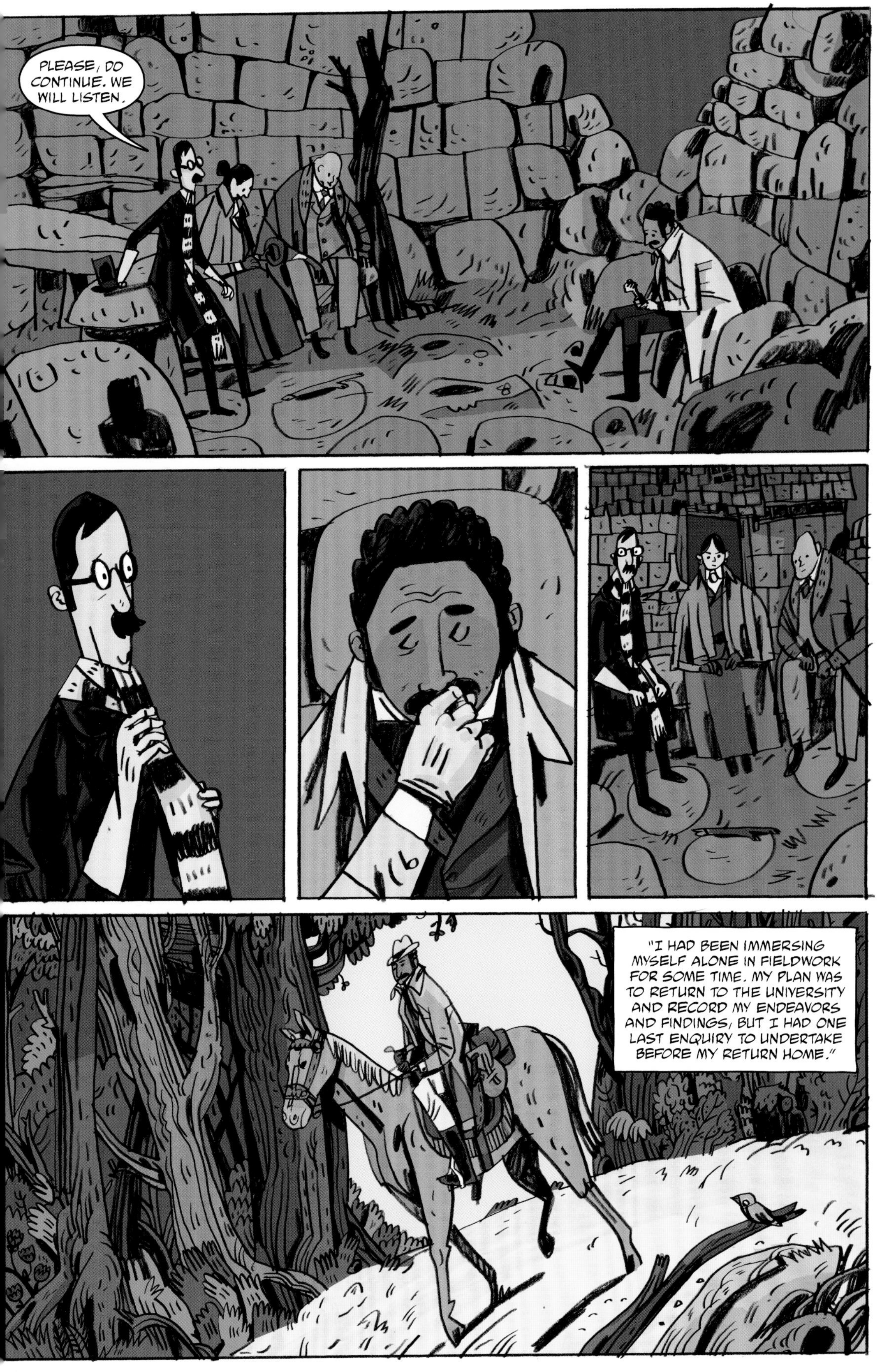
PLEASE, DO CONTINUE. WE WILL LISTEN.
"I HAD BEEN IMMERSING MYSELF ALONE IN FIELDWORK FOR SOME TIME. MY PLAN WAS TO RETURN TO THE UNIVERSITY AND RECORD MY ENDEAVORS AND FINDINGS, BUT I HAD ONE LAST ENQUIRY TO UNDERTAKE BEFORE MY RETURN HOME."

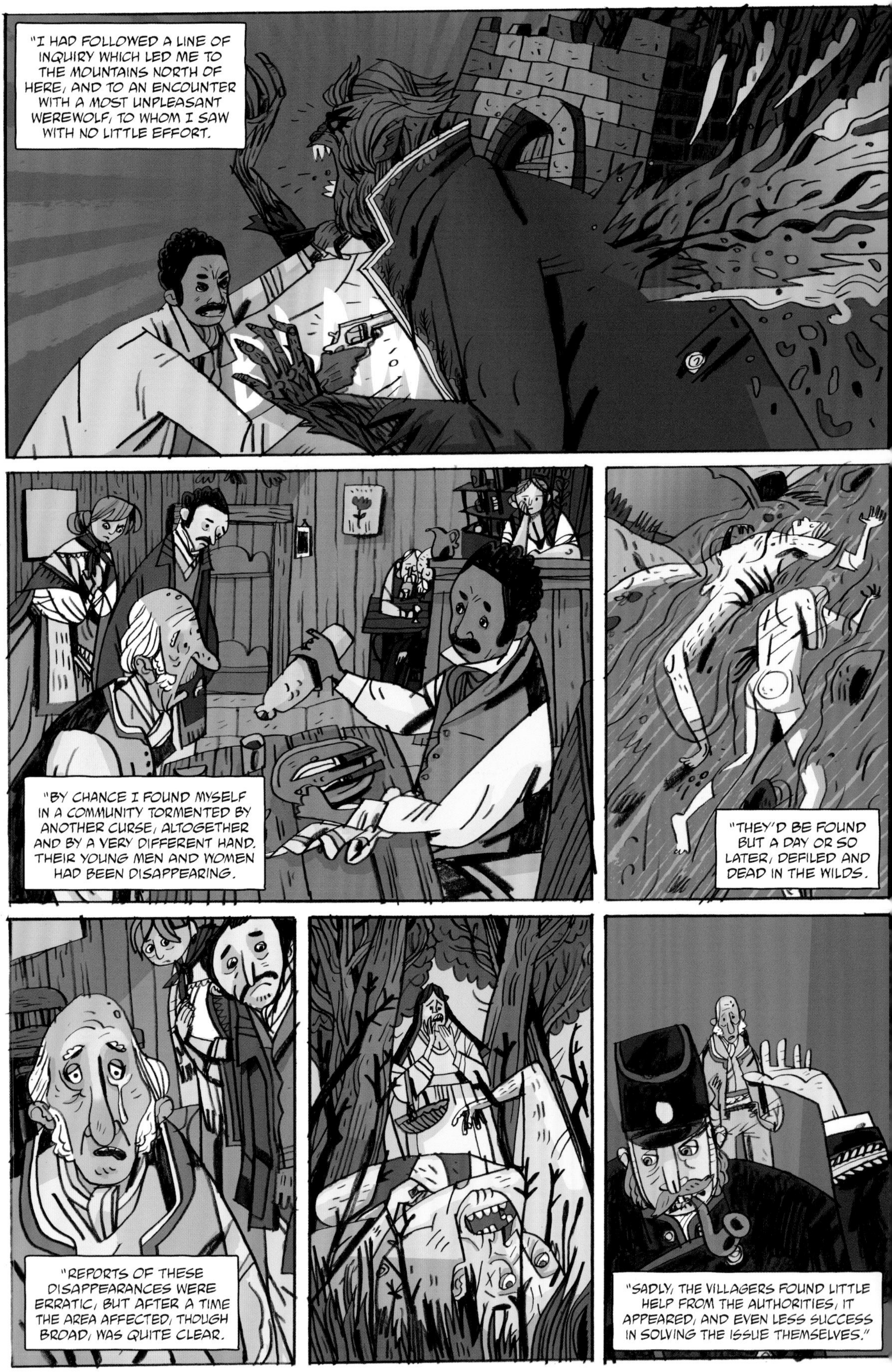
"I HAD FOLLOWED A LINE OF INQUIRY WHICH LED ME TO THE MOUNTAINS NORTH OF HERE, AND TO AN ENCOUNTER WITH A MOST UNPLEASANT WEREWOLF, TO WHOM I SAW WITH NO LITTLE EFFORT.
"BY CHANCE I FOUND MYSELF IN A COMMUNITY TORMENTED BY ANOTHER CURSE, ALTOGETHER AND BY A VERY DIFFERENT HAND. THEIR YOUNG MEN AND WOMEN HAD BEEN DISAPPEARING.
"THEY'D BE FOUND BUT A DAY OR SO LATER, DEFILED AND DEAD IN THE WILDS.
"REPORTS OF THESE DISAPPEARANCES WERE ERRATIC, BUT AFTER A TIME THE AREA AFFECTED, THOUGH BROAD, WAS QUITE CLEAR.
"SADLY, THE VILLAGERS FOUND LITTLE HELP FROM THE AUTHORITIES, IT APPEARED, AND EVEN LESS SUCCESS IN SOLVING THE ISSUE THEMSELVES."

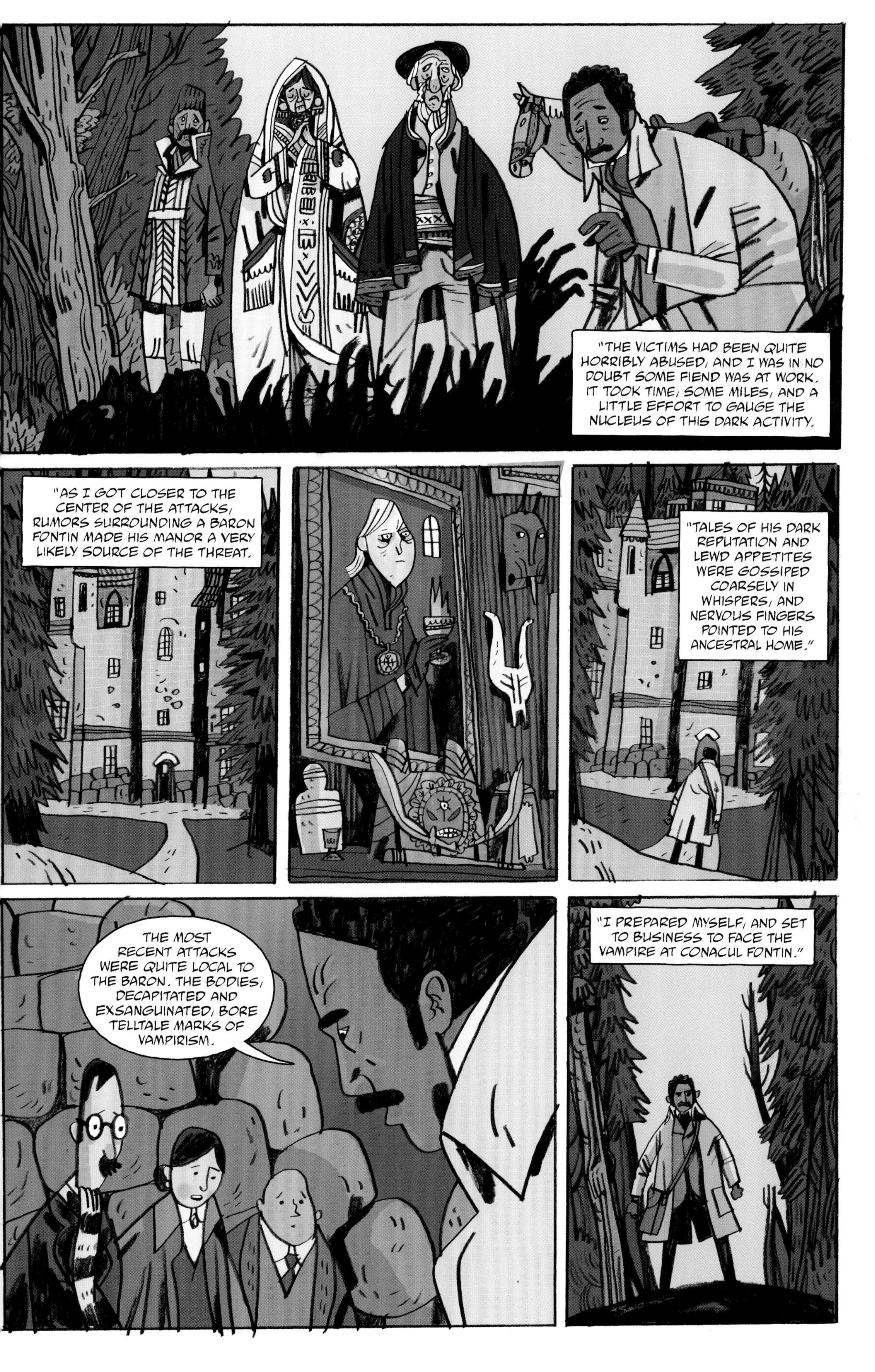
"THE VICTIMS HAD BEEN QUITE HORRIBLY ABUSED, AND I WAS IN NO DOUBT SOME FIEND WAS AT WORK. IT TOOK TIME, SOME MILES, AND A LITTLE EFFORT TO GAUGE THE NUCLEUS OF THIS DARK ACTIVITY.
"AS I GOT CLOSER TO THE CENTER OF THE ATTACKS, RUMORS SURROUNDING A BARON FONTIN MADE HIS MANOR A VERY LIKELY SOURCE OF THE THREAT.
"TALES OF HIS DARK REPUTATION AND LEWD APPETITES WERE GOSSIPED COARSELY IN WHISPERS, AND NERVOUS FINGERS POINTED TO HIS ANCESTRAL HOME."
THE MOST RECENT ATTACKS WERE QUITE LOCAL TO THE BARON. THE BODIES, DECAPITATED AND EXSANGUINATED, BORE TELLTALE MARKS OF VAMPIRISM.
"I PREPARED MYSELF, AND SET TO BUSINESS TO FACE THE VAMPIRE AT CONACUL FONTIN."

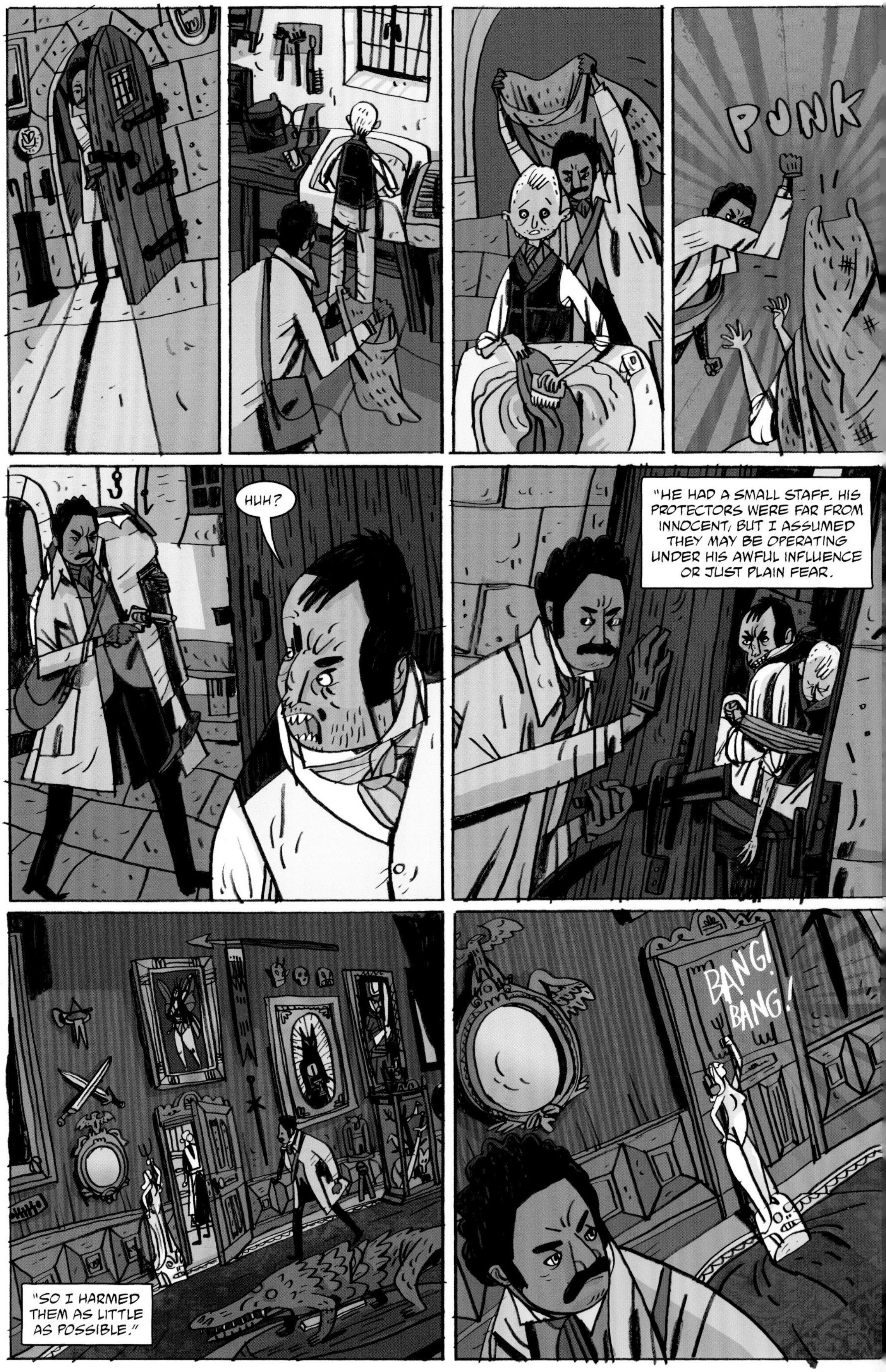
PUNK
HUH?
"HE HAD A SMALL STAFF. HIS PROTECTORS WERE FAR FROM INNOCENT, BUT I ASSUMED THEY MAY BE OPERATING UNDER HIS AWFUL INFLUENCE OR JUST PLAIN FEAR.
"SO I HARMED THEM AS LITTLE AS POSSIBLE."
BANG! BANG!

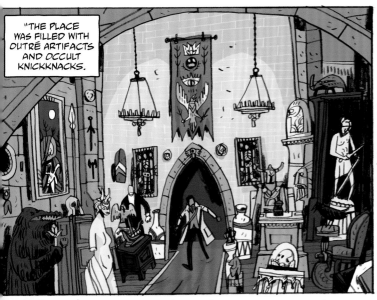

"THE PLACE WAS FILLED WITH OUTRÉ ARTIFACTS AND OCCULT KNICKKNACKS."

"IT WAS A DIABOLIC LAIR."

GRAB!

KNOCK

DONK!

KRASH

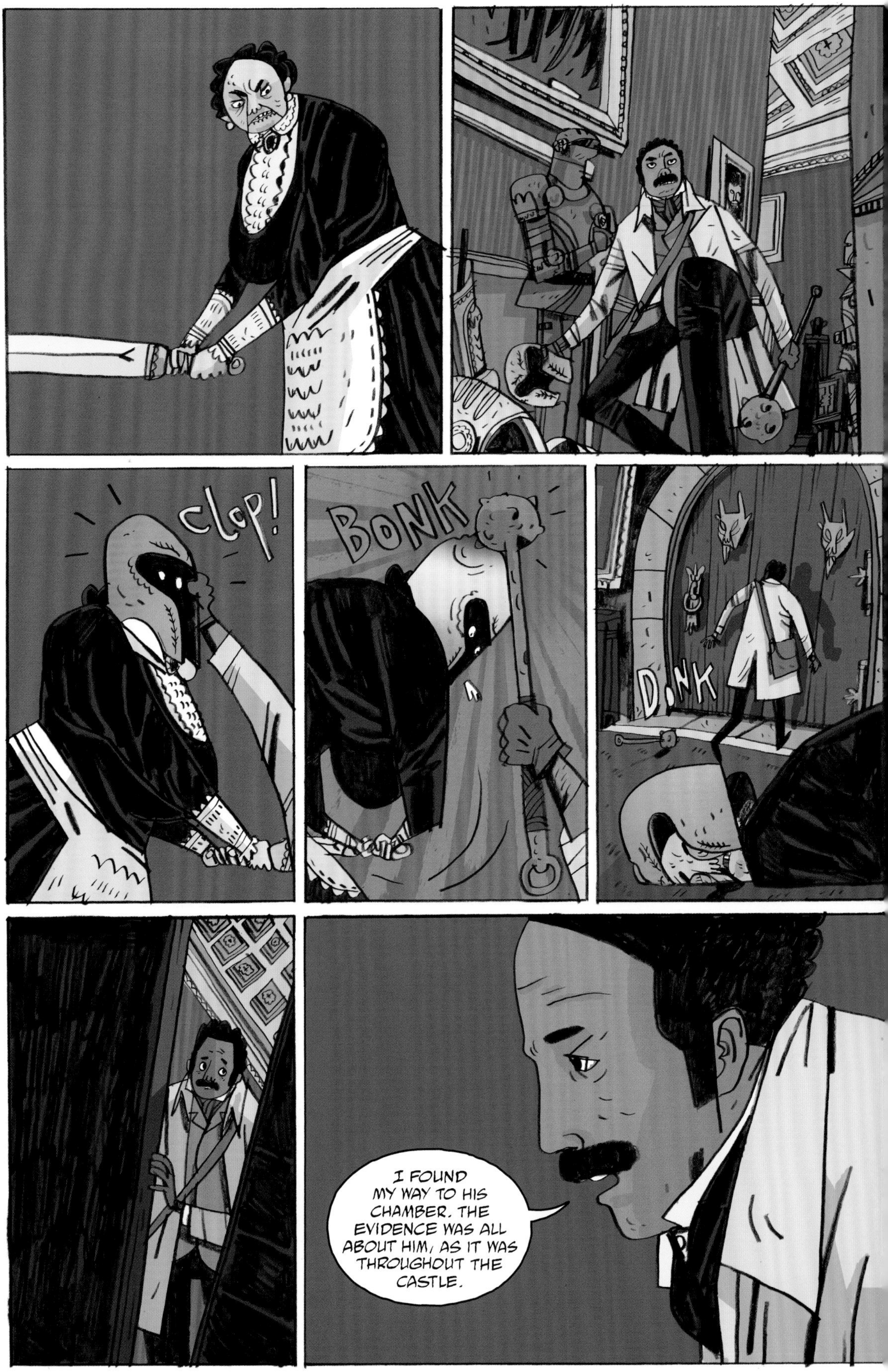
clop!
BONK
DONK
I FOUND MY WAY TO HIS CHAMBER. THE EVIDENCE WAS ALL ABOUT HIM, AS IT WAS THROUGHOUT THE CASTLE.

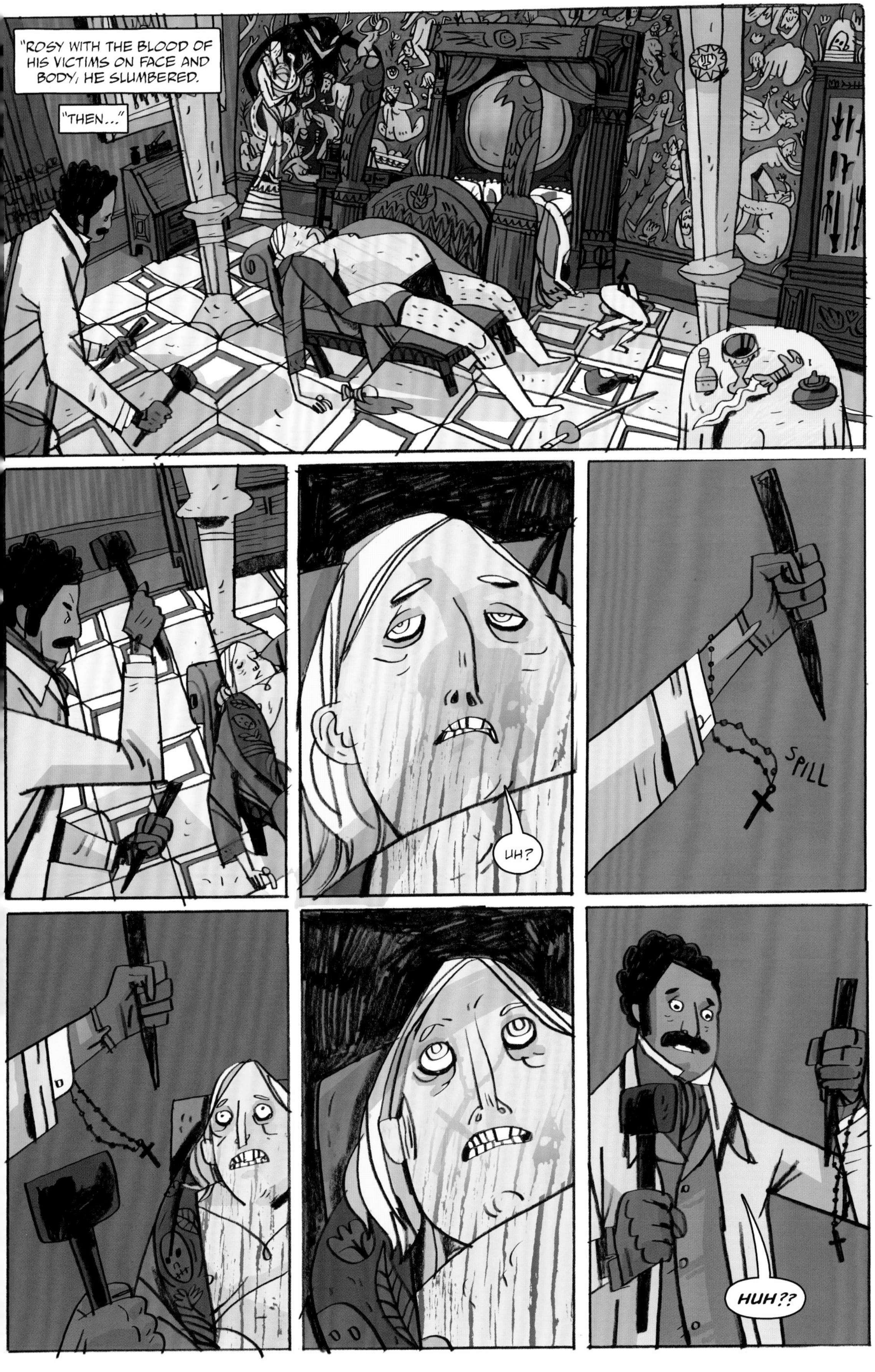
"ROSY WITH THE BLOOD OF HIS VICTIMS ON FACE AND BODY, HE SLUMBERED.
"THEN..."
UH?
SPILL
HUH??

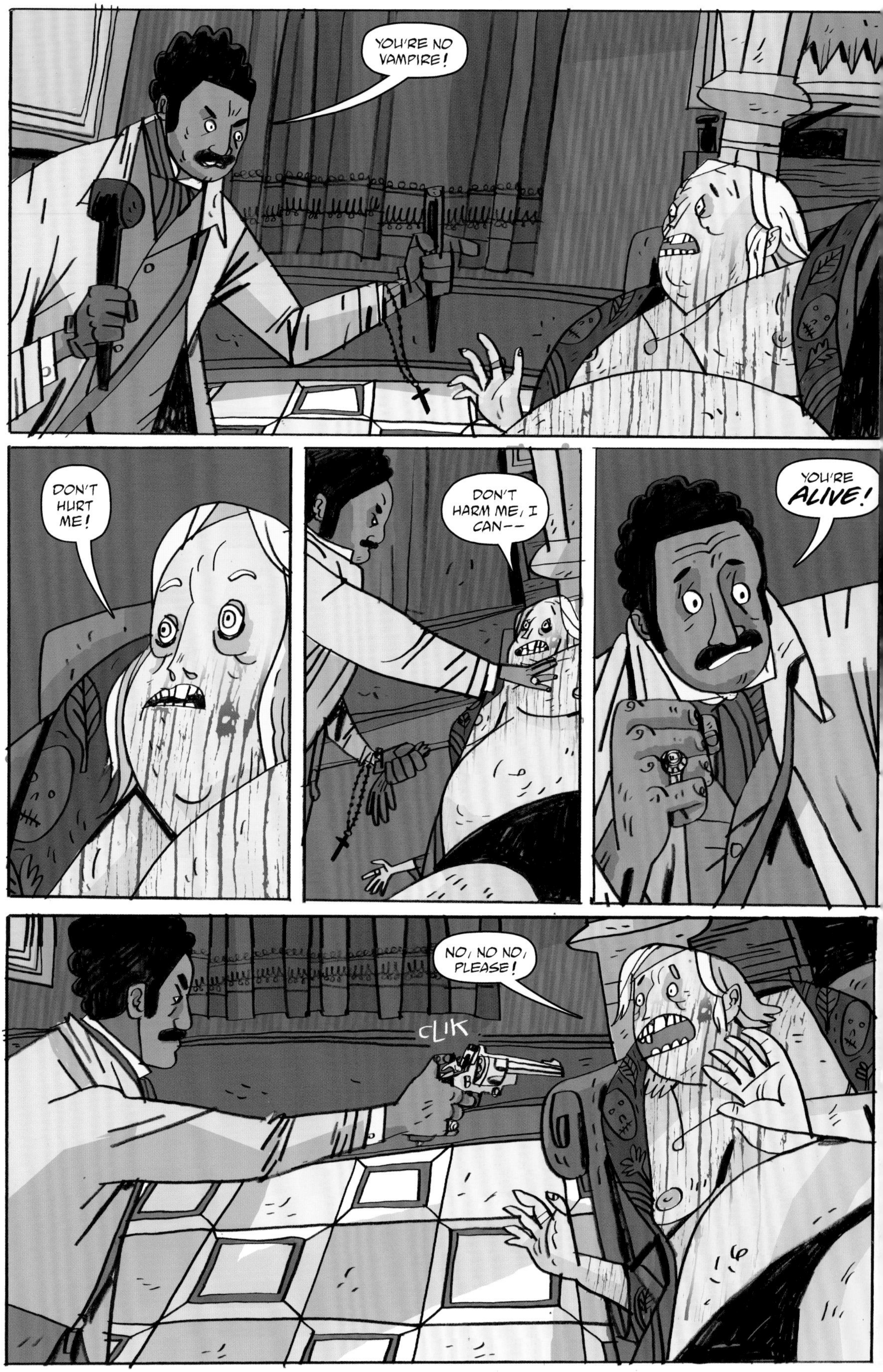
YOU'RE NO VAMPIRE!
DON'T HURT ME!
DON'T HARM ME, I CAN--
YOU'RE ALIVE!
NO, NO NO, PLEASE!
CLIK

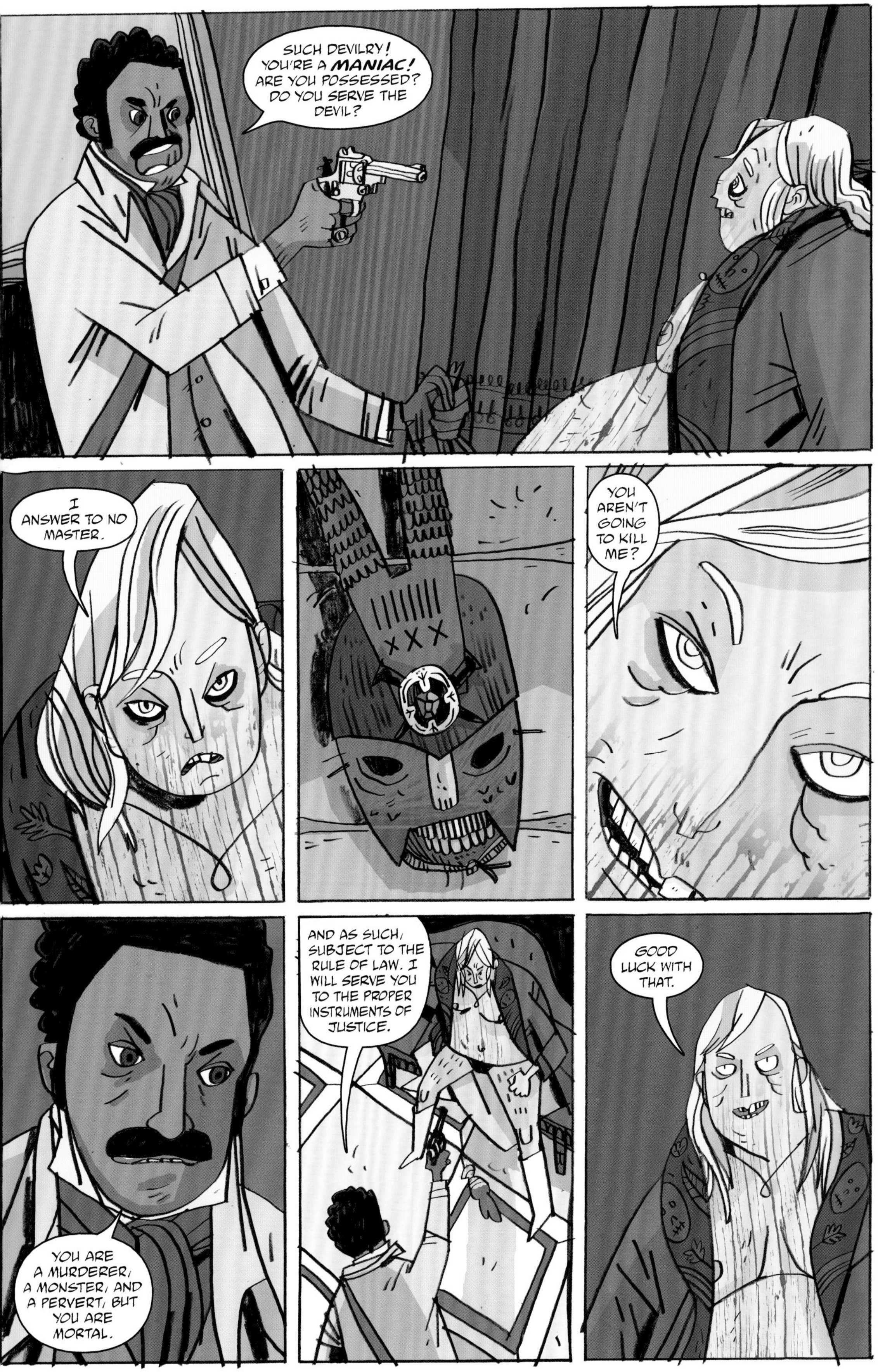
SUCH DEVILRY! YOU'RE A MANIAC! ARE YOU POSSESSED? DO YOU SERVE THE DEVIL?
I ANSWER TO NO MASTER.
YOU AREN'T GOING TO KILL ME?
YOU ARE A MURDERER, A MONSTER, AND A PERVERT, BUT YOU ARE MORTAL.
AND AS SUCH, SUBJECT TO THE RULE OF LAW. I WILL SERVE YOU TO THE PROPER INSTRUMENTS OF JUSTICE.
GOOD LUCK WITH THAT.

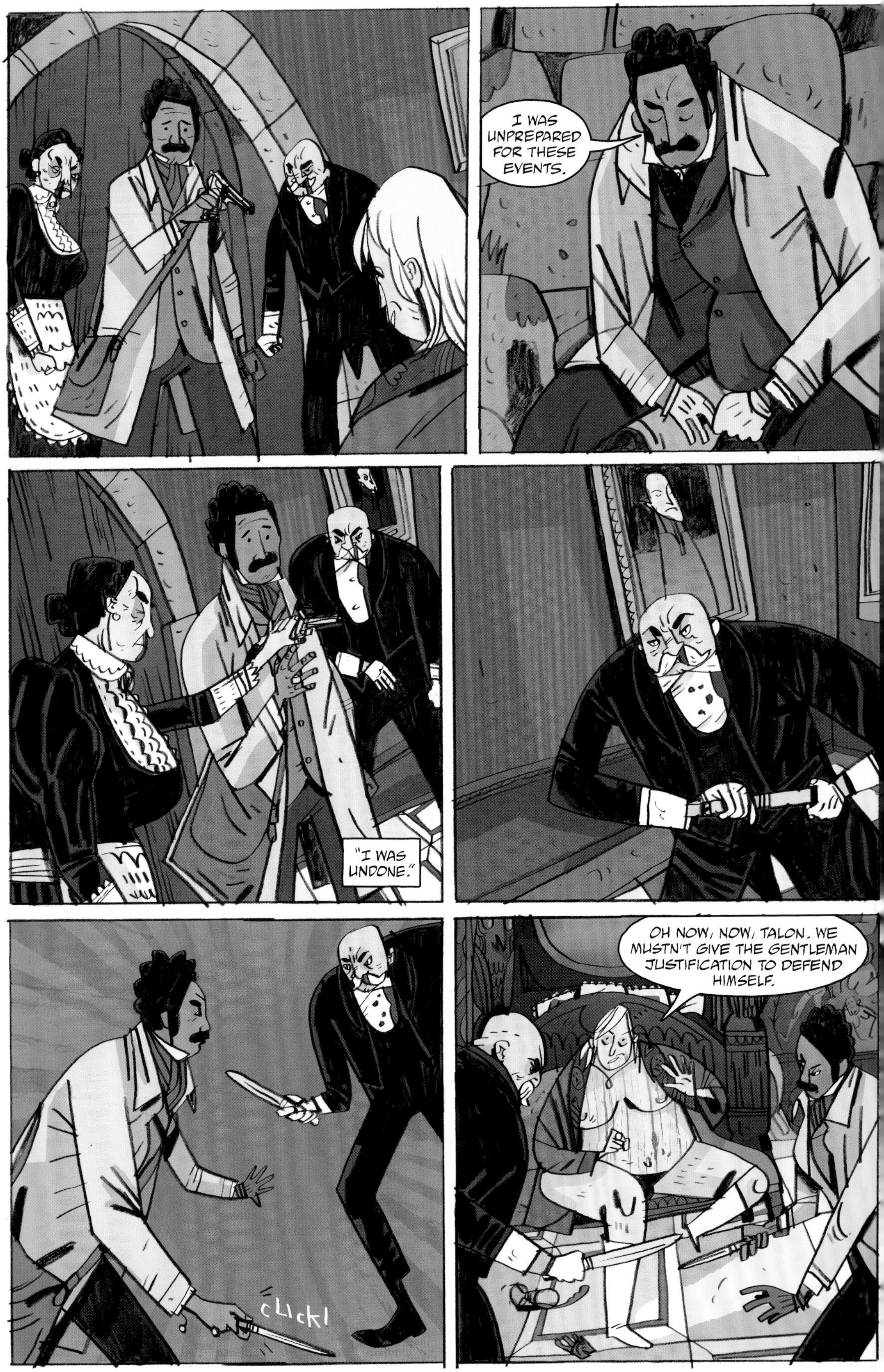
I WAS UNPREPARED FOR THESE EVENTS.
"I WAS UNDONE."
CLICK!
OH NOW, NOW, TALON. WE MUSTN'T GIVE THE GENTLEMAN JUSTIFICATION TO DEFEND HIMSELF.

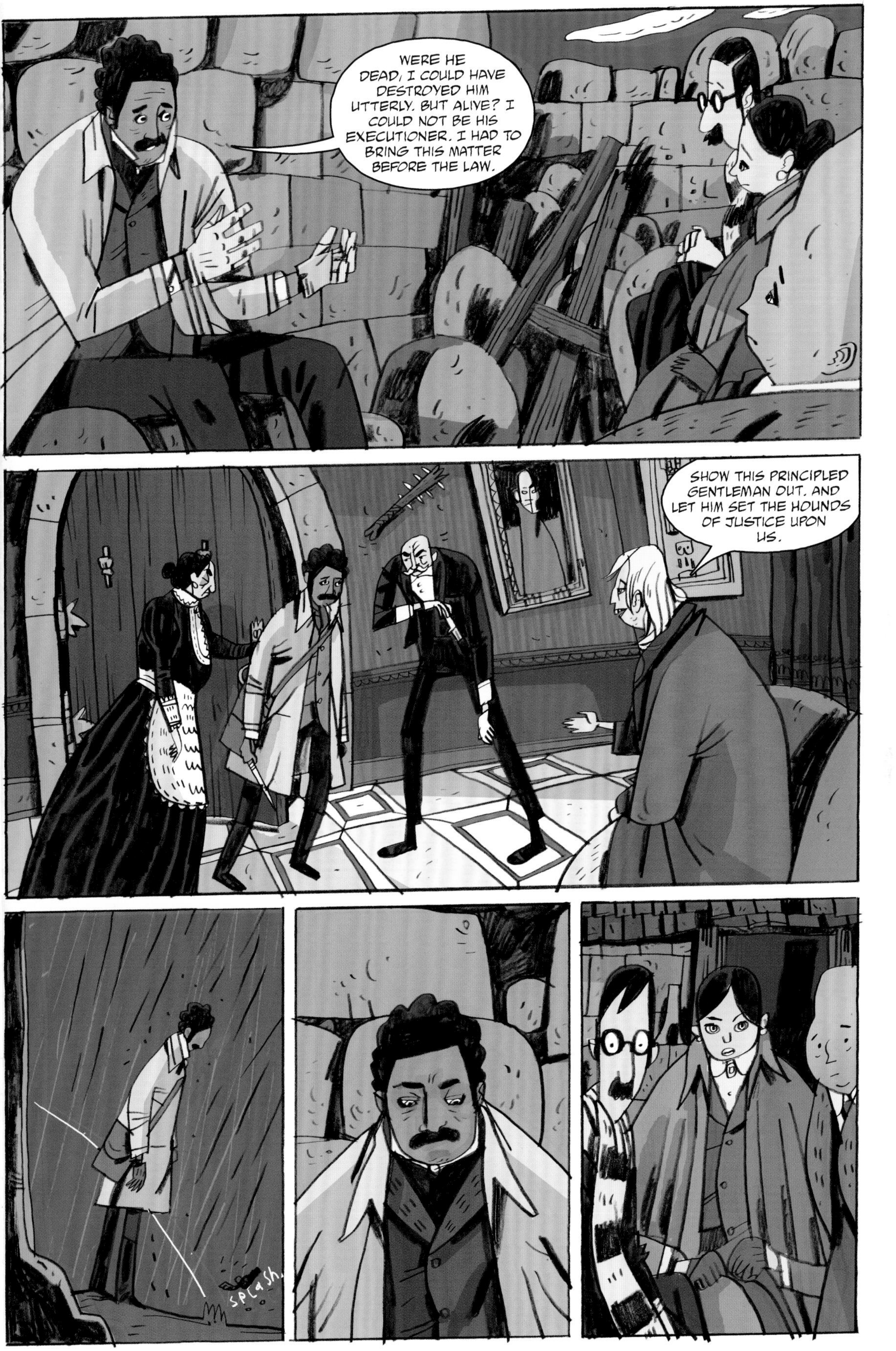
WERE HE DEAD, I COULD HAVE DESTROYED HIM UTTERLY. BUT ALIVE? I COULD NOT BE HIS EXECUTIONER. I HAD TO BRING THIS MATTER BEFORE THE LAW.
SHOW THIS PRINCIPLED GENTLEMAN OUT. AND LET HIM SET THE HOUNDS OF JUSTICE UPON US.
sPLash.

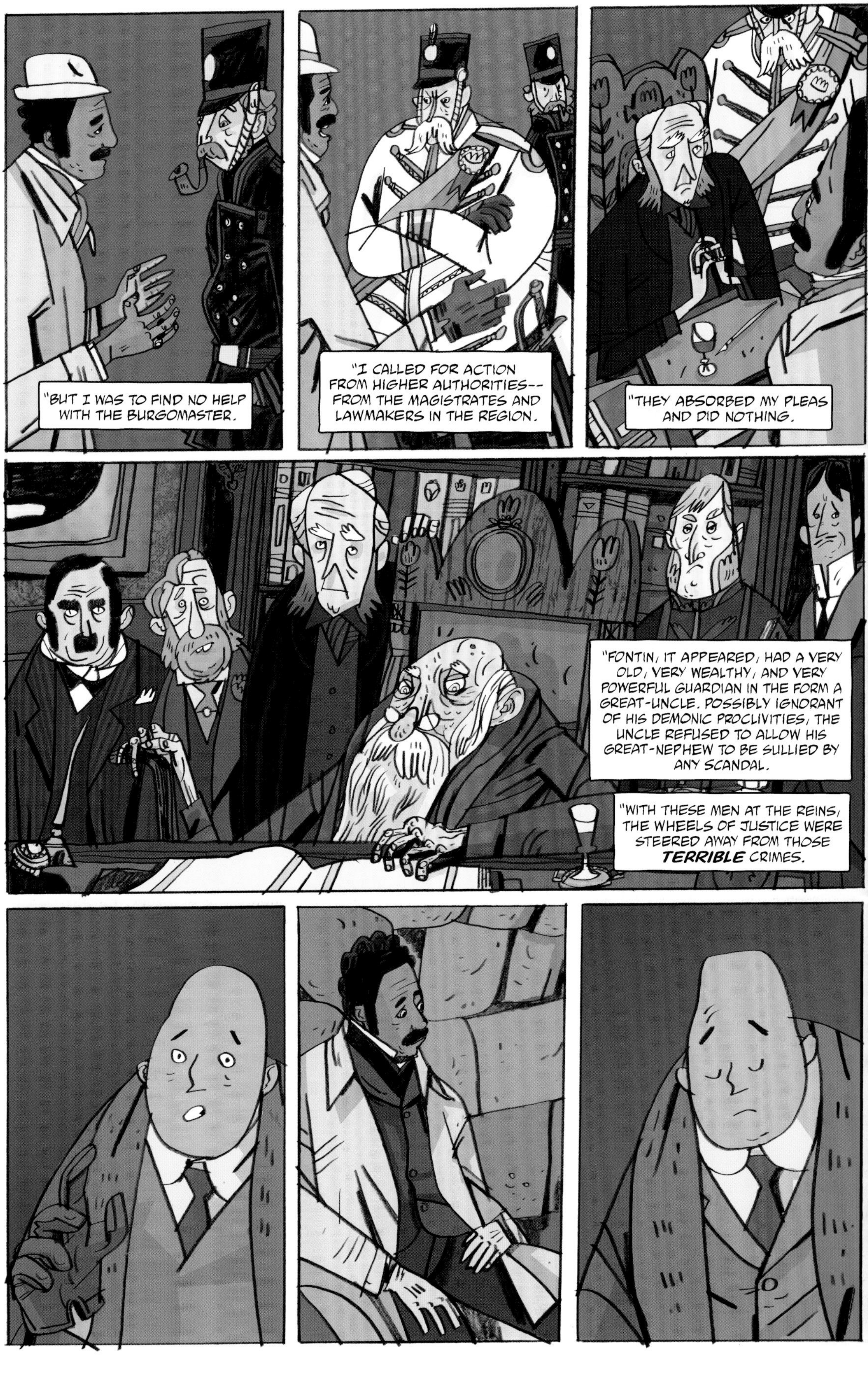
"BUT I WAS TO FIND NO HELP WITH THE BURGOMASTER.
"I CALLED FOR ACTION FROM HIGHER AUTHORITIES-- FROM THE MAGISTRATES AND LAWMAKERS IN THE REGION.
"THEY ABSORBED MY PLEAS AND DID NOTHING.
"FONTIN, IT APPEARED, HAD A VERY OLD, VERY WEALTHY, AND VERY POWERFUL GUARDIAN IN THE FORM A GREAT-UNCLE. POSSIBLY IGNORANT OF HIS DEMONIC PROCLIVITIES, THE UNCLE REFUSED TO ALLOW HIS GREAT-NEPHEW TO BE SULLIED BY ANY SCANDAL.
"WITH THESE MEN AT THE REINS, THE WHEELS OF JUSTICE WERE STEERED AWAY FROM THOSE TERRIBLE CRIMES.

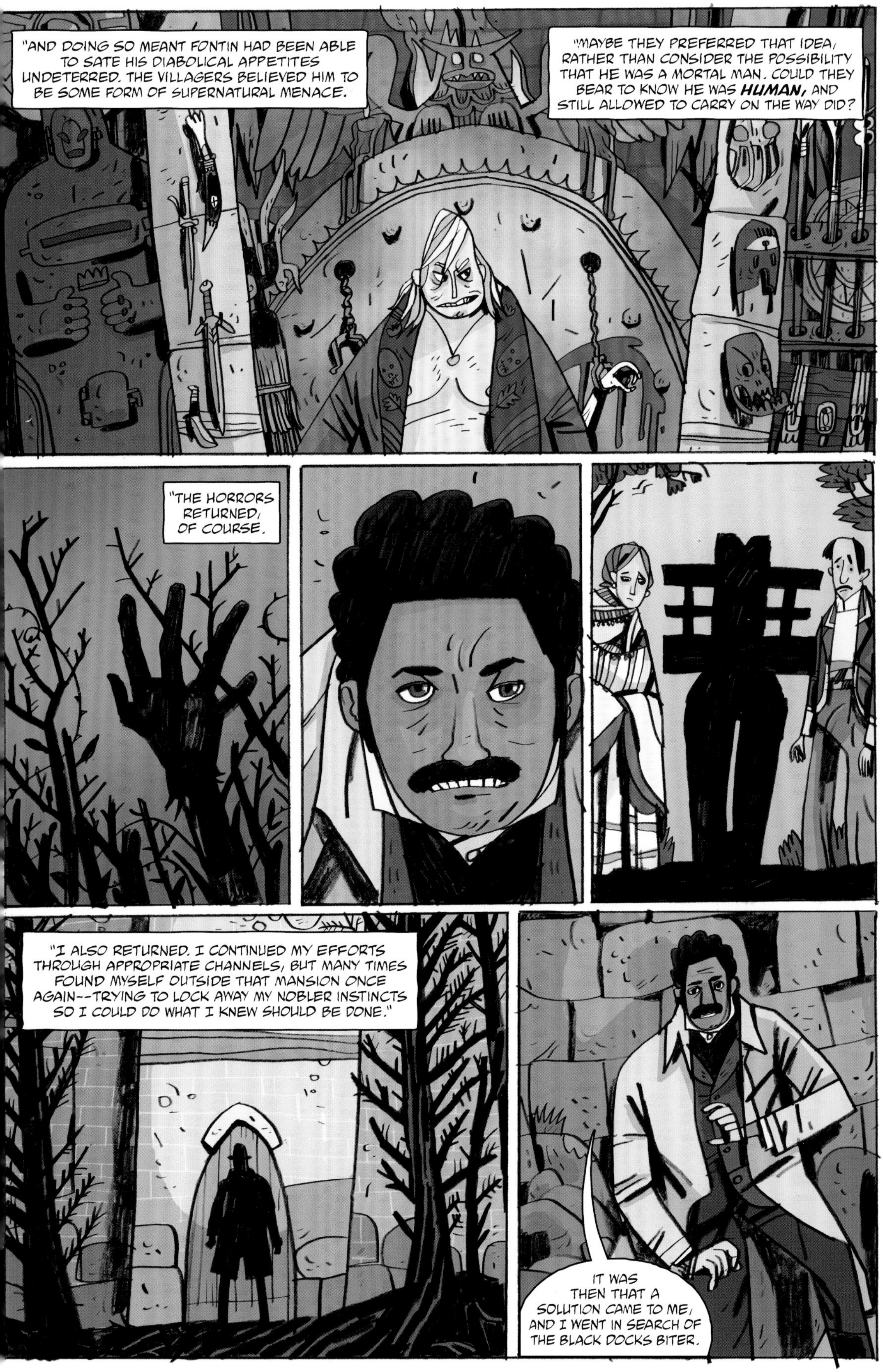
"AND DOING SO MEANT FONTIN HAD BEEN ABLE TO SATE HIS DIABOLICAL APPETITES UNDETERRED. THE VILLAGERS BELIEVED HIM TO BE SOME FORM OF SUPERNATURAL MENACE.
"MAYBE THEY PREFERRED THAT IDEA, RATHER THAN CONSIDER THE POSSIBILITY THAT HE WAS A MORTAL MAN. COULD THEY BEAR TO KNOW HE WAS HUMAN, AND STILL ALLOWED TO CARRY ON THE WAY DID?
"THE HORRORS RETURNED, OF COURSE.
"I ALSO RETURNED. I CONTINUED MY EFFORTS THROUGH APPROPRIATE CHANNELS, BUT MANY TIMES FOUND MYSELF OUTSIDE THAT MANSION ONCE AGAIN--TRYING TO LOCK AWAY MY NOBLER INSTINCTS SO I COULD DO WHAT I KNEW SHOULD BE DONE."
IT WAS THEN THAT A SOLUTION CAME TO ME, AND I WENT IN SEARCH OF THE BLACK DOCKS BITER.

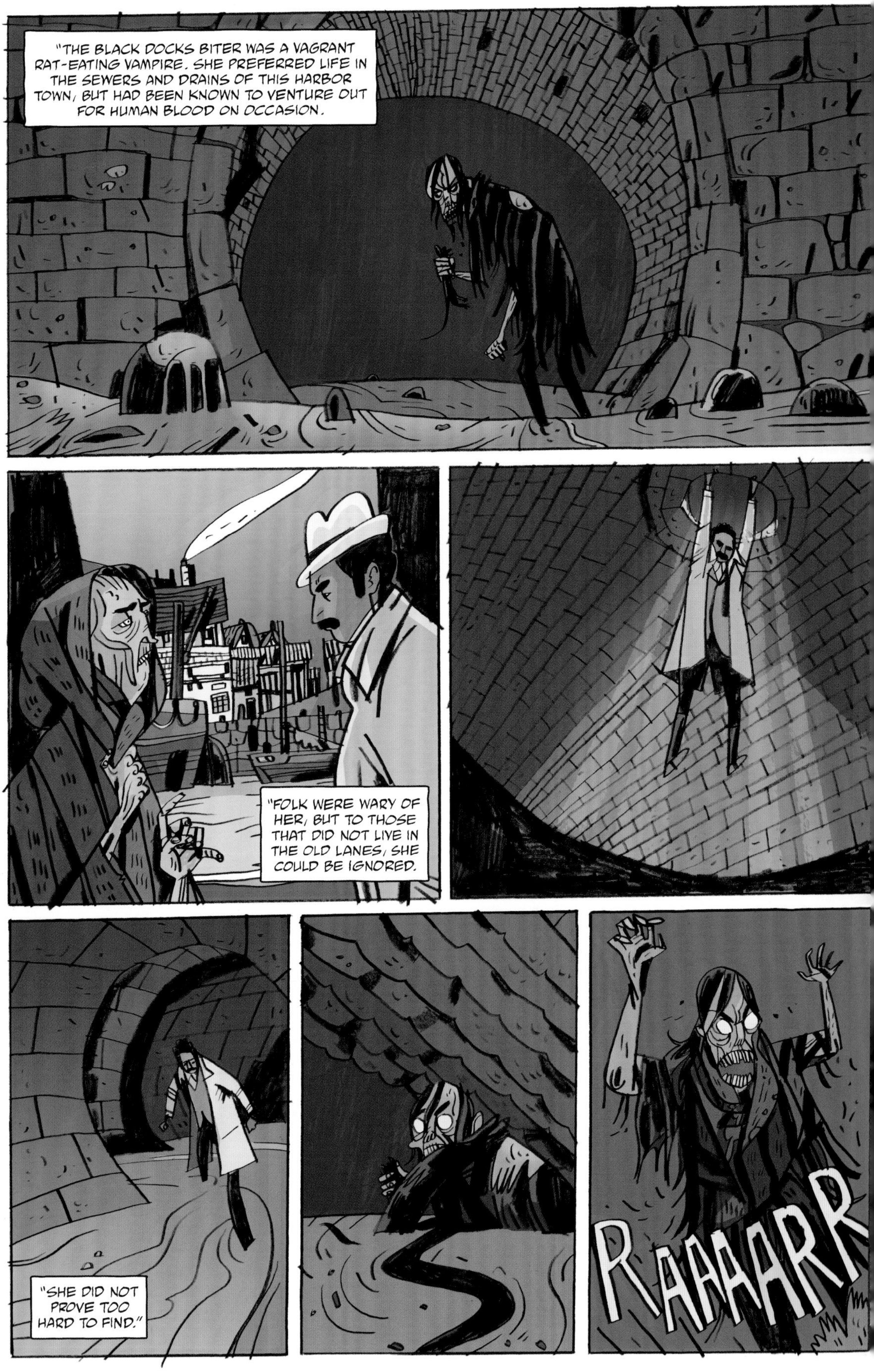
"THE BLACK DOCKS BITER WAS A VAGRANT RAT-EATING VAMPIRE. SHE PREFERRED LIFE IN THE SEWERS AND DRAINS OF THIS HARBOR TOWN, BUT HAD BEEN KNOWN TO VENTURE OUT FOR HUMAN BLOOD ON OCCASION.
"FOLK WERE WARY OF HER, BUT TO THOSE THAT DID NOT LIVE IN THE OLD LANES, SHE COULD BE IGNORED.
"SHE DID NOT PROVE TOO HARD TO FIND."
RAAAARR

HISSSSSSSS!!

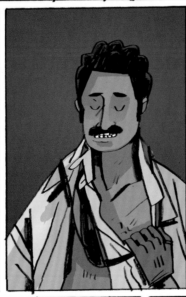

click

SHUNK!!

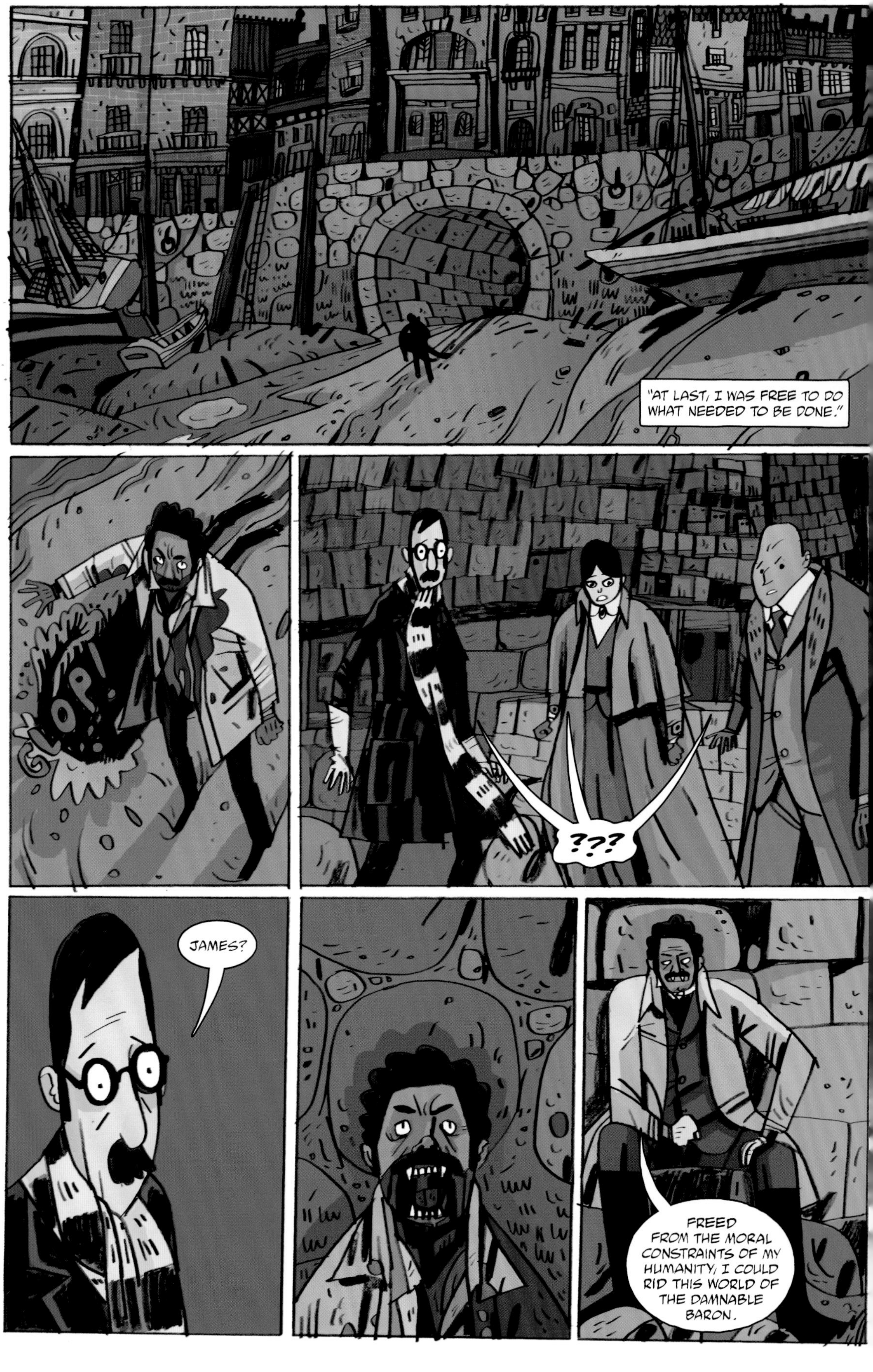
"AT LAST, I WAS FREE TO DO WHAT NEEDED TO BE DONE."
GLOP!
???
JAMES?
FREED FROM THE MORAL CONSTRAINTS OF MY HUMANITY, I COULD RID THIS WORLD OF THE DAMNABLE BARON.

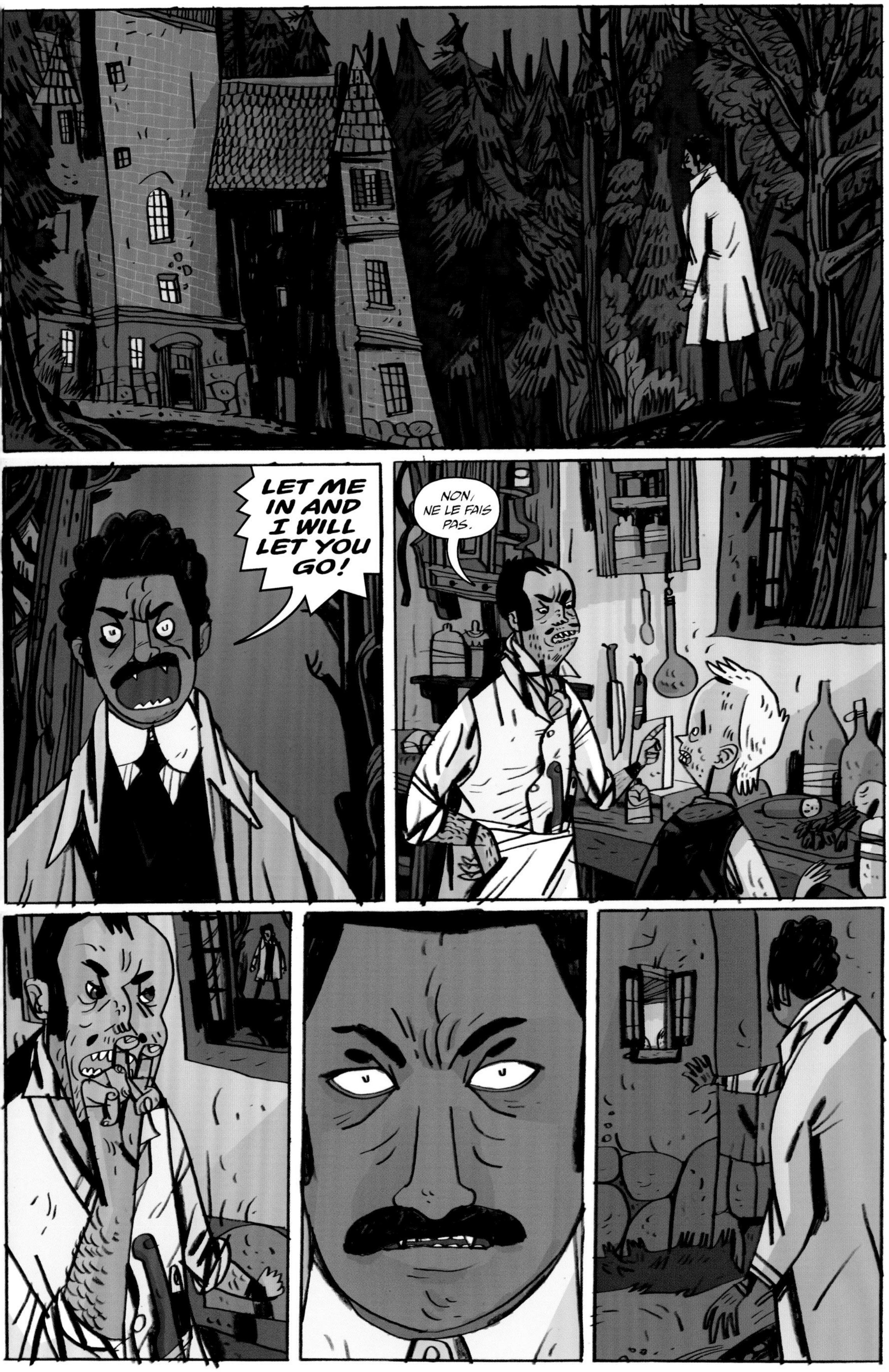
LET ME IN AND I WILL LET YOU GO!
NON, NE LE FAIS PAS.

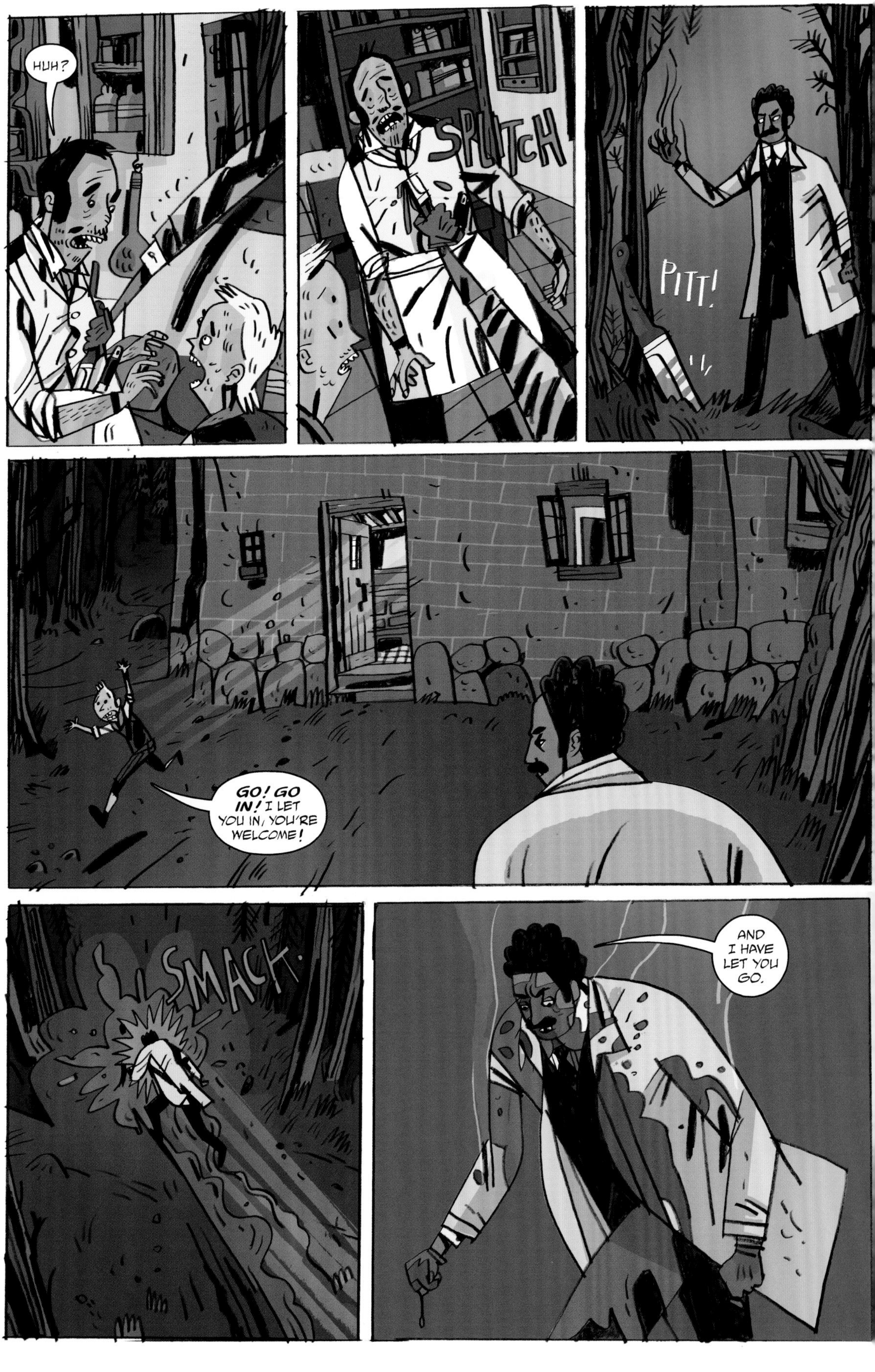
HUH?
SPLUTCH
PITT!
GO! GO IN! I LET YOU IN, YOU'RE WELCOME!
SMACK.
AND I HAVE LET YOU GO.

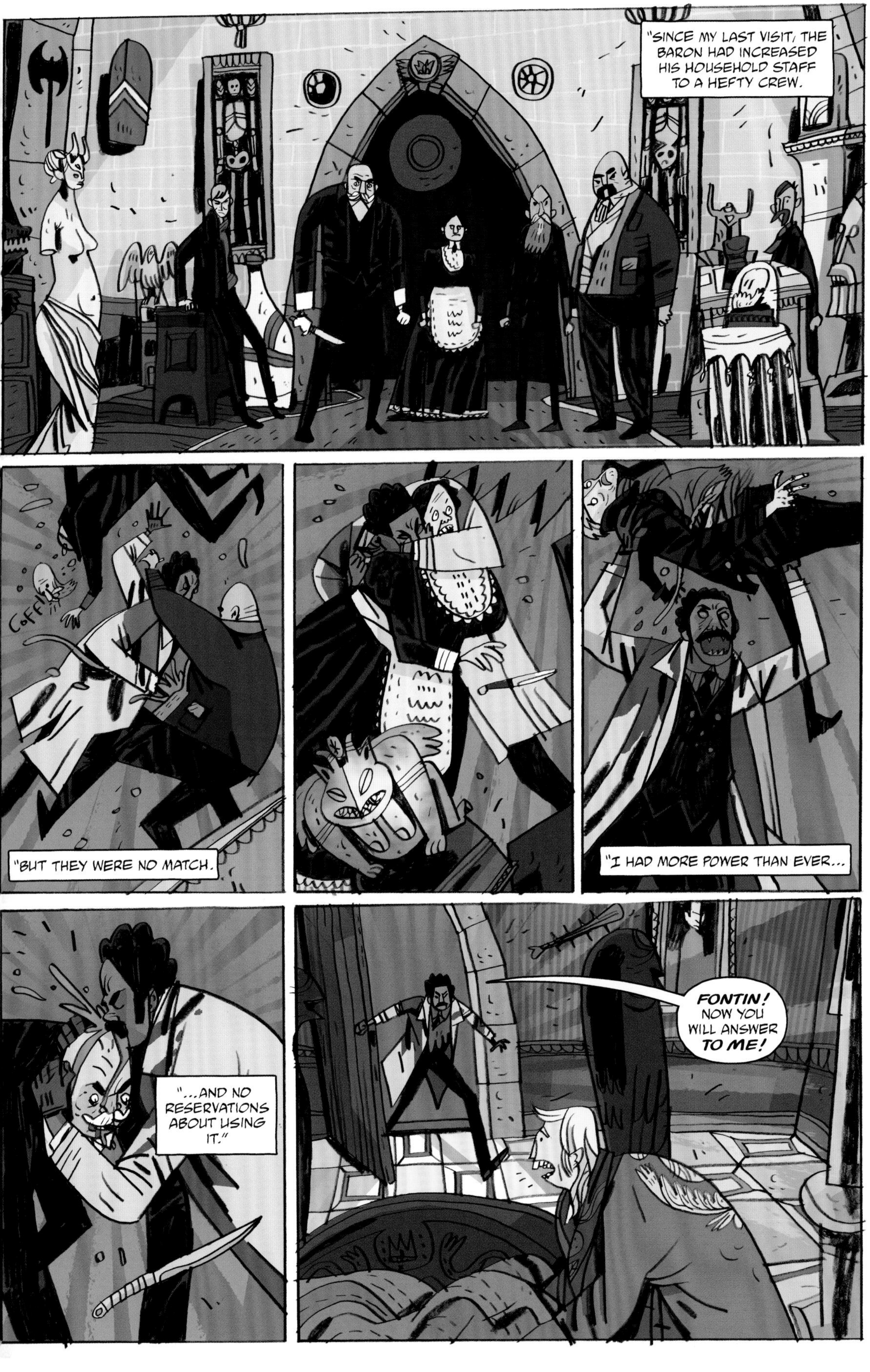
"SINCE MY LAST VISIT, THE BARON HAD INCREASED HIS HOUSEHOLD STAFF TO A HEFTY CREW.
COFF!
"BUT THEY WERE NO MATCH.
"I HAD MORE POWER THAN EVER...
"...AND NO RESERVATIONS ABOUT USING IT."
FONTIN! NOW YOU WILL ANSWER TO ME!

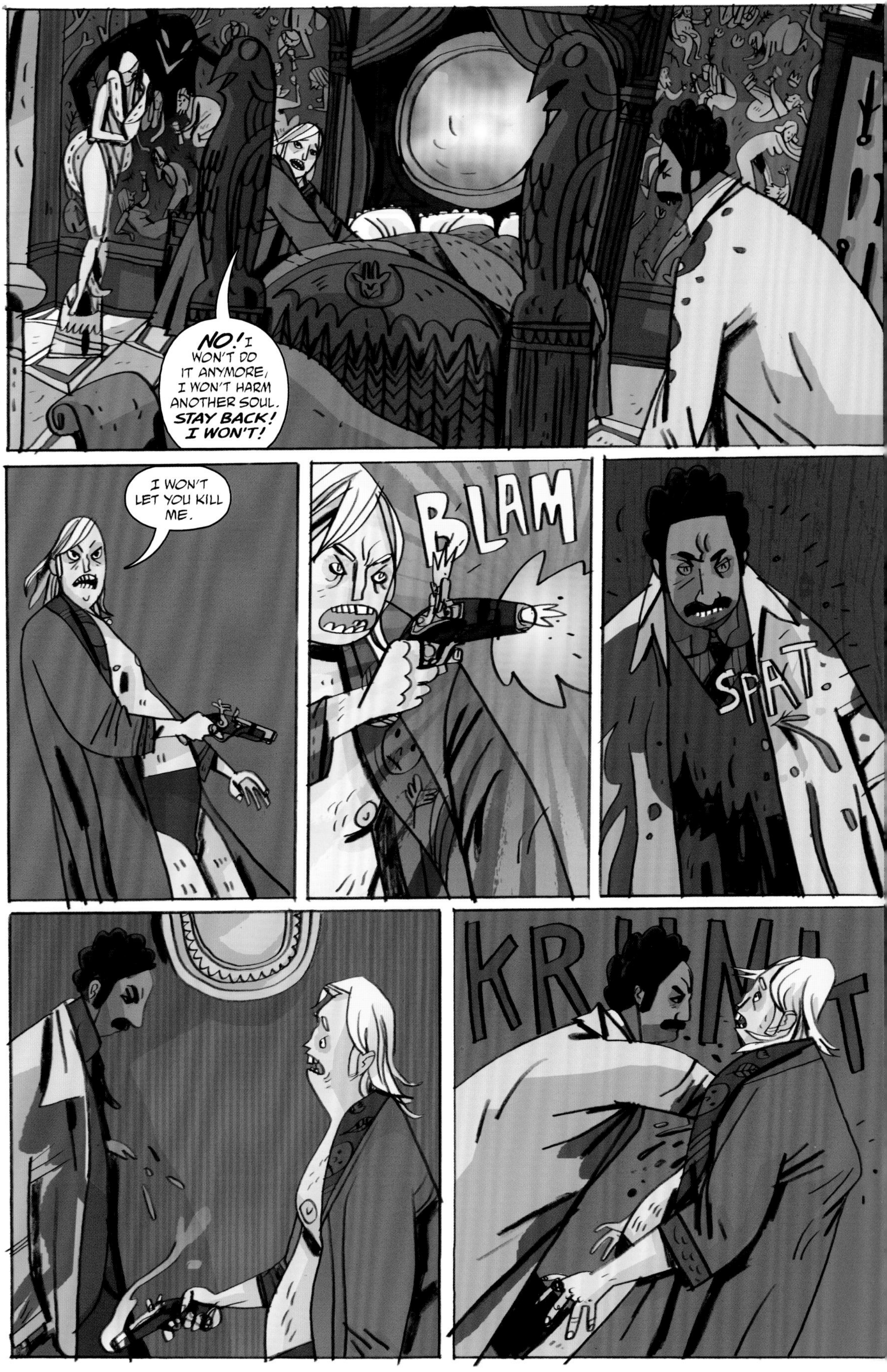
NO! I WON'T DO IT ANYMORE, I WON'T HARM ANOTHER SOUL. STAY BACK! I WON'T!
I WON'T LET YOU KILL ME.
BLAM
SPAT

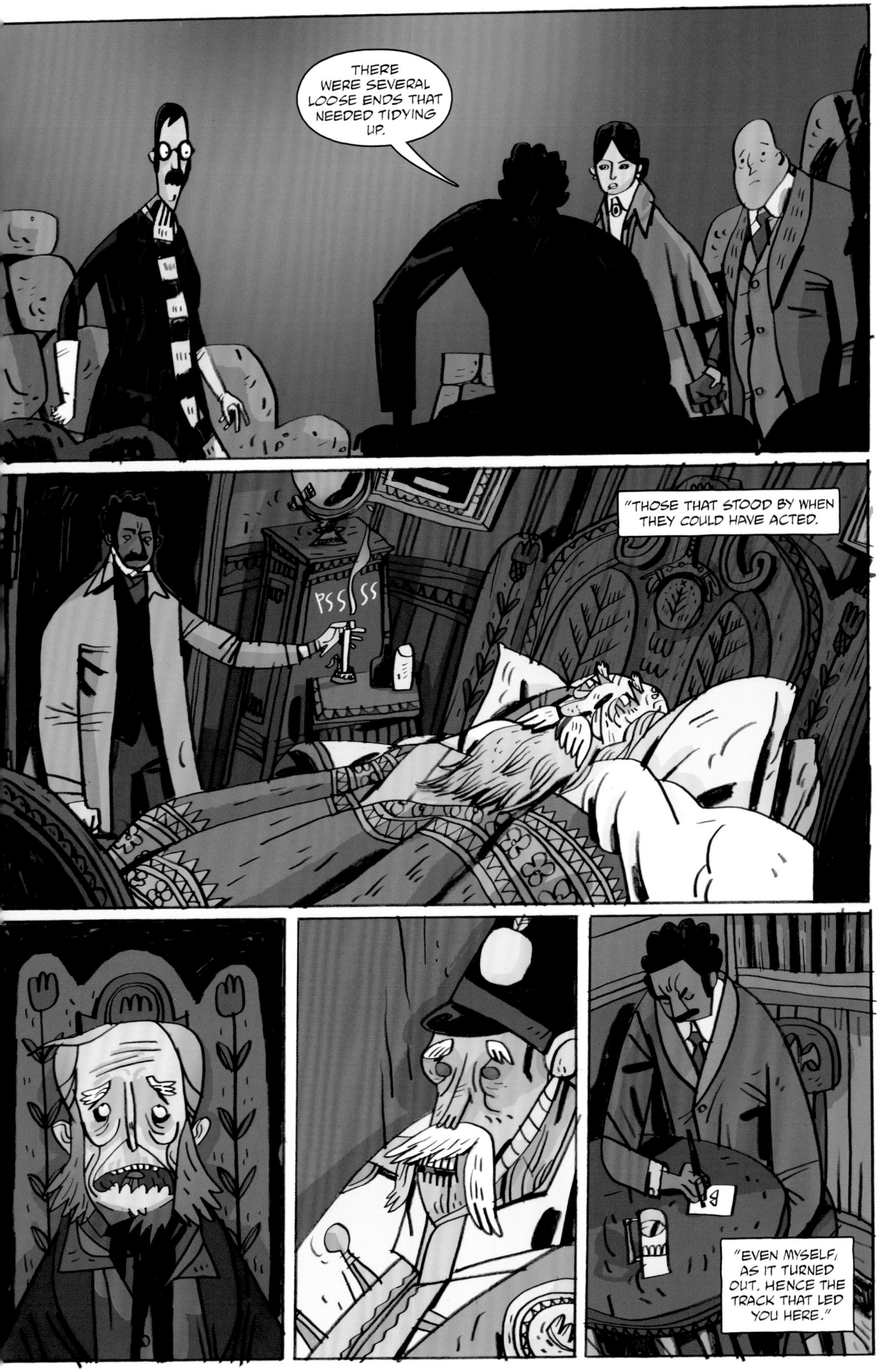

THERE WERE SEVERAL LOOSE ENDS THAT NEEDED TIDYING UP.
"THOSE THAT STOOD BY WHEN THEY COULD HAVE ACTED.
PSSSSS
"EVEN MYSELF, AS IT TURNED OUT. HENCE THE TRACK THAT LED YOU HERE."

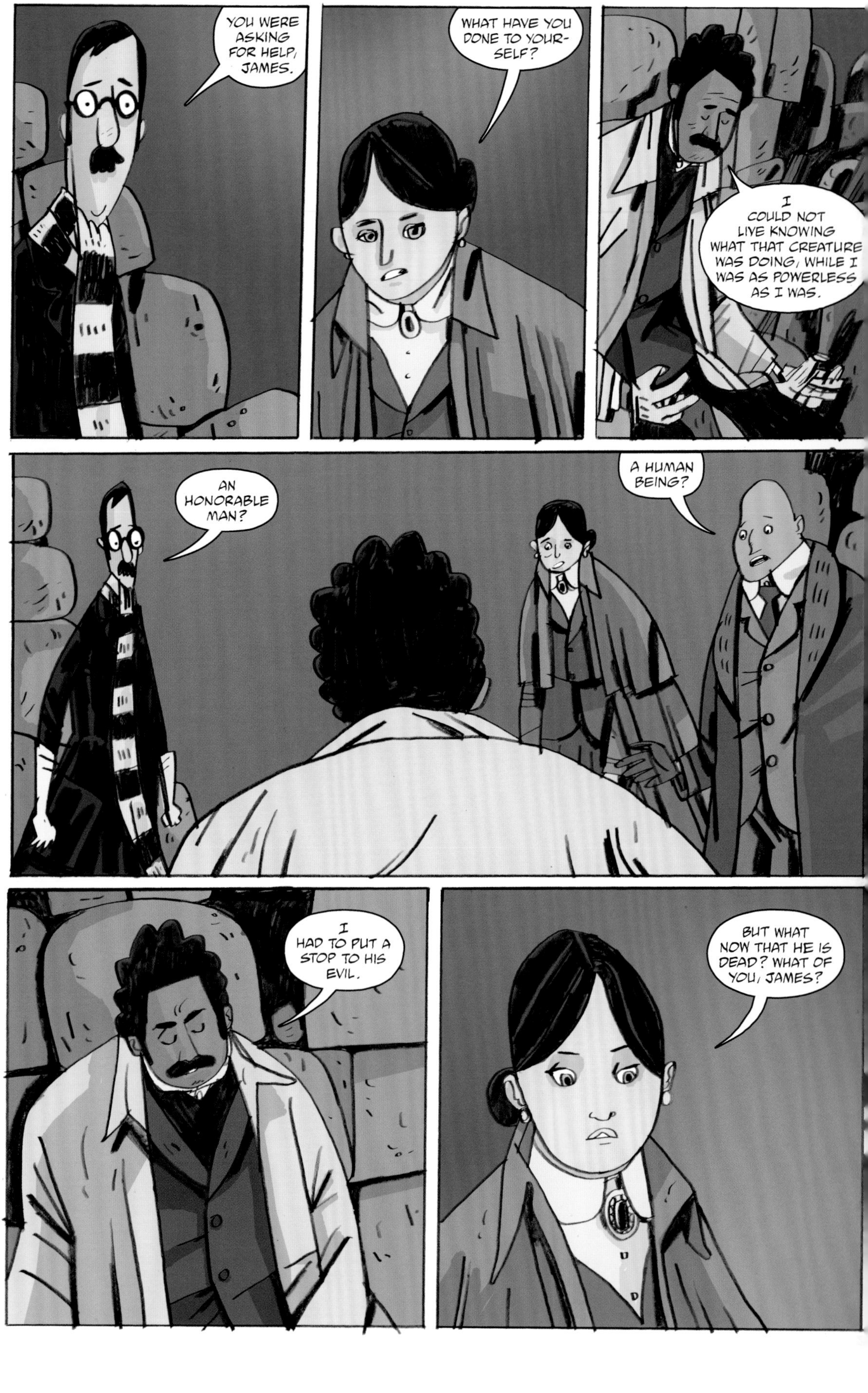

YOU WERE ASKING FOR HELP, JAMES.
WHAT HAVE YOU DONE TO YOURSELF?
I COULD NOT LIVE KNOWING WHAT THAT CREATURE WAS DOING, WHILE I WAS AS POWERLESS AS I WAS.
AN HONORABLE MAN?
A HUMAN BEING?
I HAD TO PUT A STOP TO HIS EVIL.
BUT WHAT NOW THAT HE IS DEAD? WHAT OF YOU, JAMES?

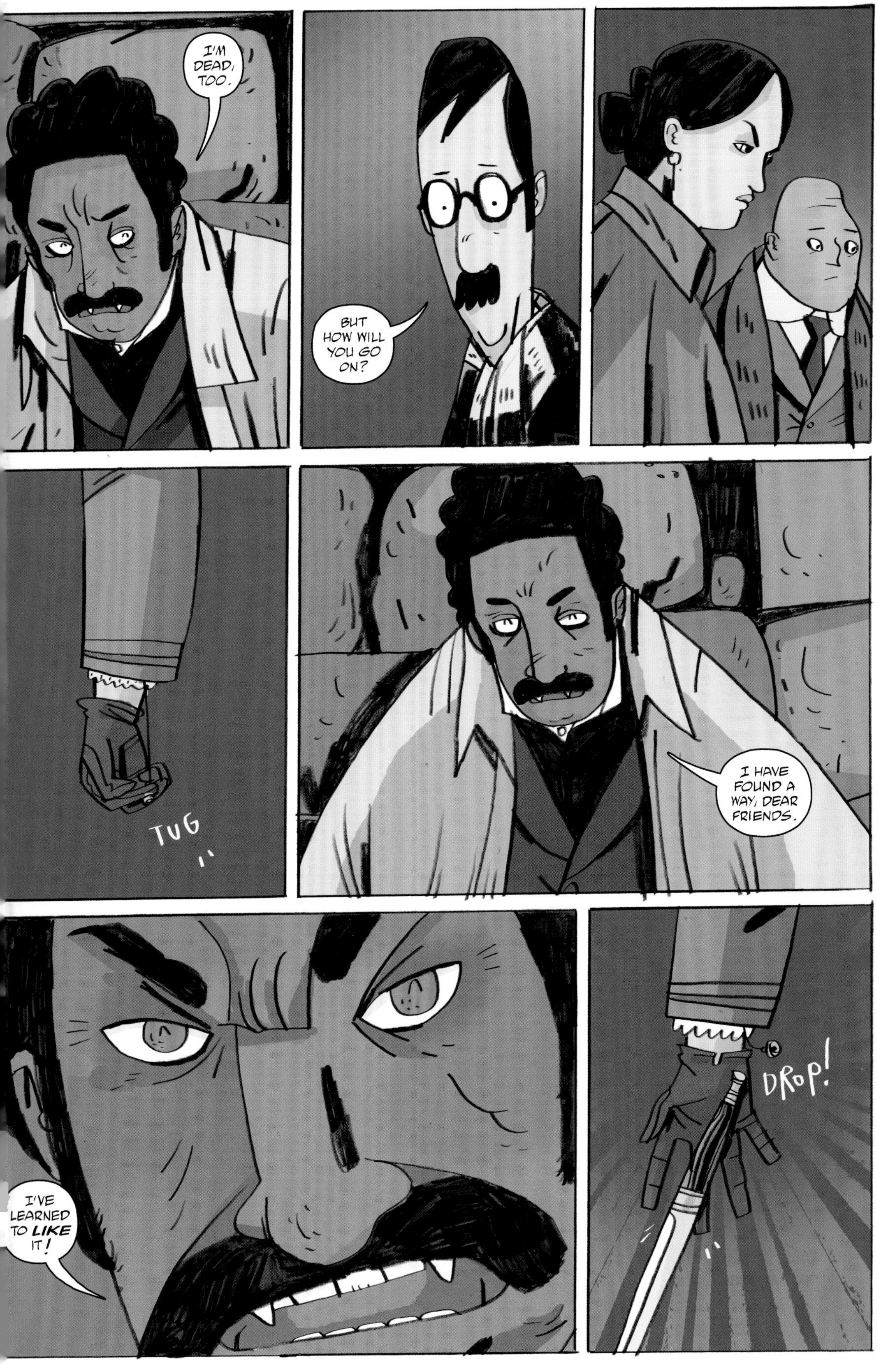
I'M DEAD, TOO.
BUT HOW WILL YOU GO ON?
TUG
I HAVE FOUND A WAY, DEAR FRIENDS.
I'VE LEARNED TO **LIKE** IT!
DROP!

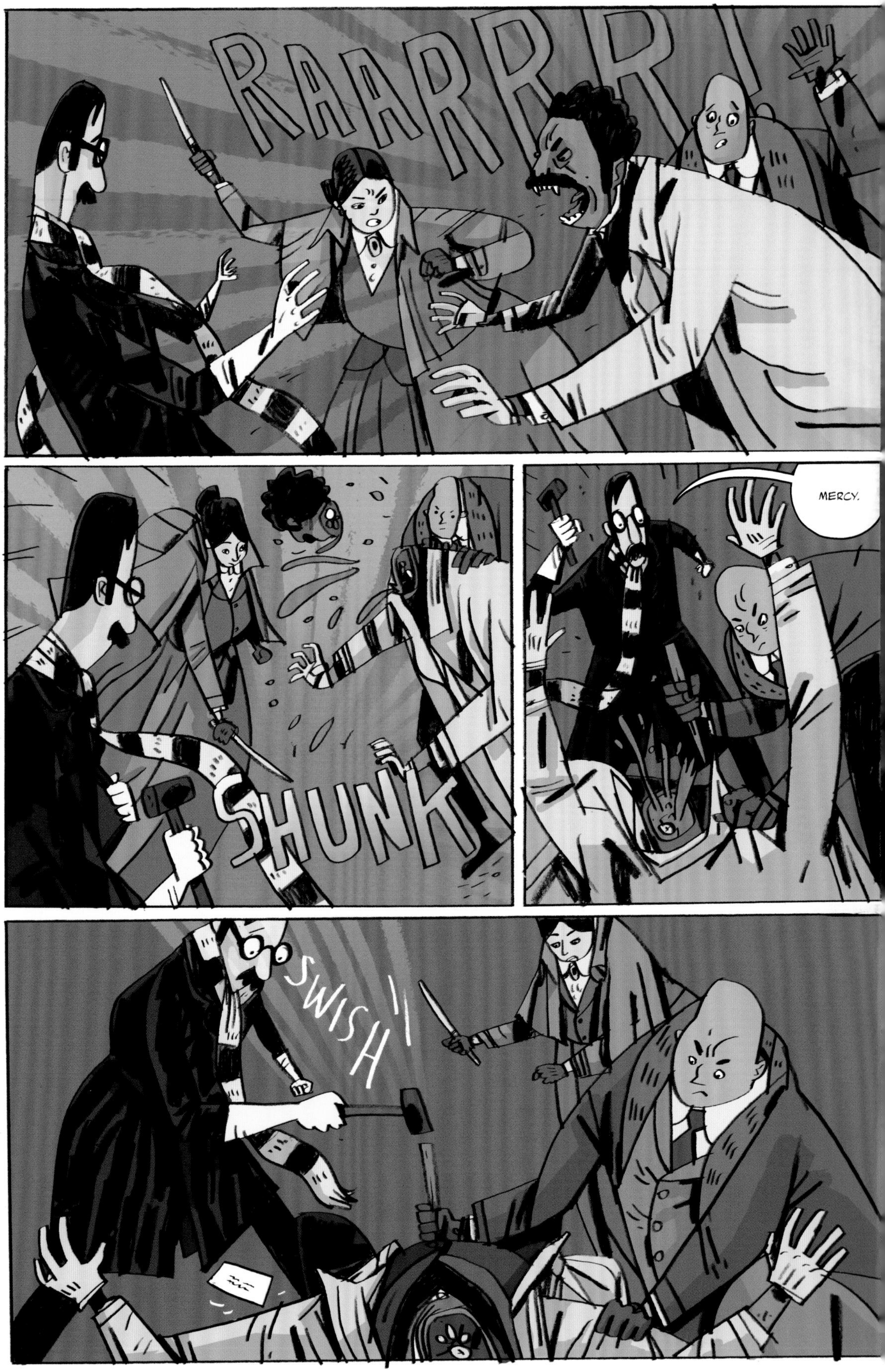
RAARRR!
SHUNK
MERCY.
SWISH

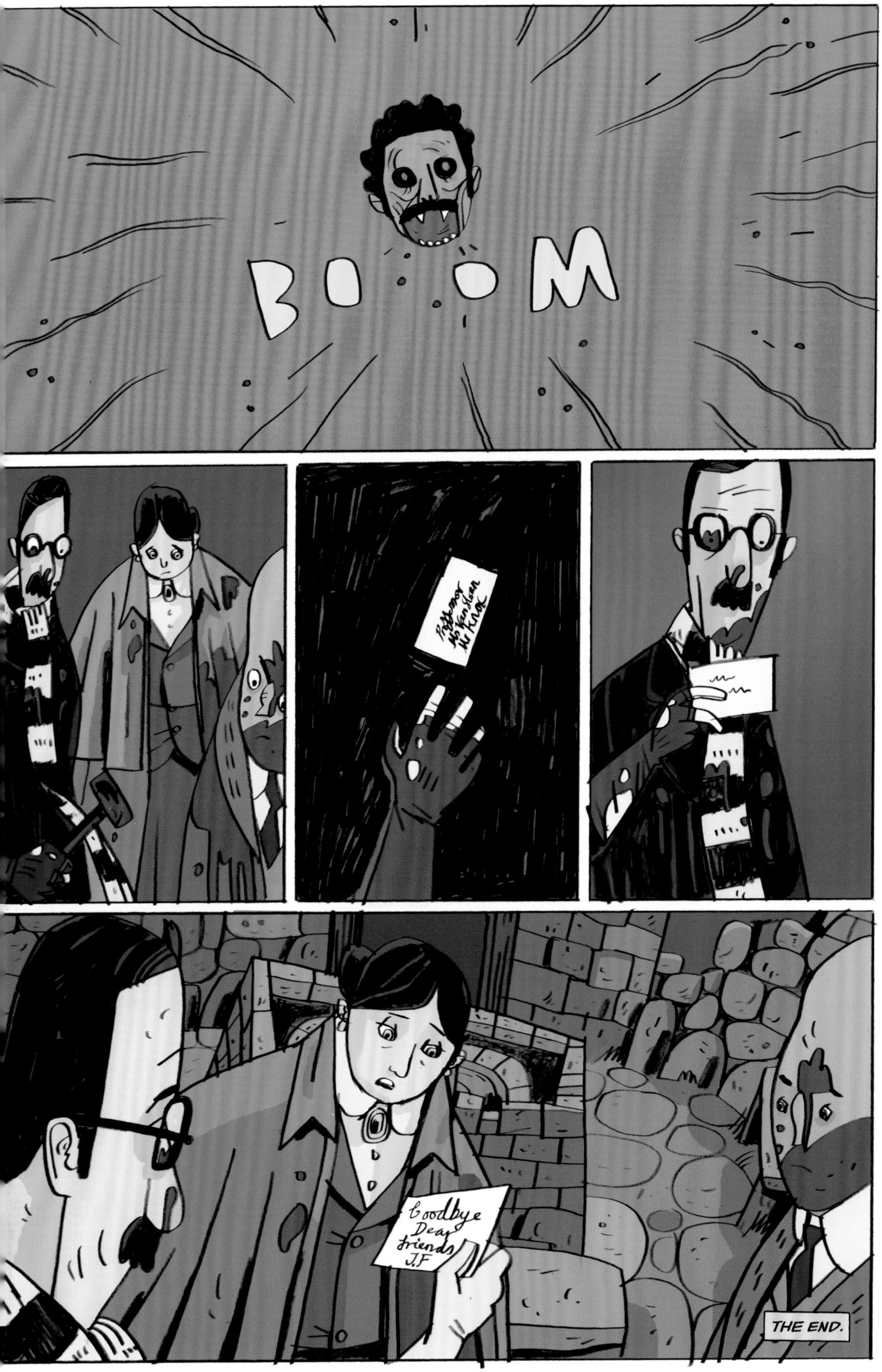
BOOM
Professor
Ms Van Sloan
Mr Knox
Goodbye Dear friends J.F
THE END.

# RECOMMENDED READING

**OUR ENCOUNTERS WITH EVIL**
*Story by Mike Mignola and Warwick Johnson-Cadwell*
*Art by Warwick Johnson-Cadwell*
*978-1-50671-166-9 • $17.99*

**MR. HIGGINS COMES HOME**
*Story by Mike Mignola*
*Art by Warwick Johnson-Cadwell*
*978-1-50670-466-1 • $14.99*

**HELLBOY IN HELL LIBRARY EDITION**
*Story and art by Mike Mignola*
*978-1-50670-363-3 • $49.99*

**HELLBOY: INTO THE SILENT SEA**
*Story by Mike Mignola and Gary Gianni*
*Art by Gary Gianni*
*978-1-50670-143-1 • $14.99*

**THE AMAZING SCREW-ON HEAD AND OTHER CURIOUS OBJECTS**
*Story and art by Mike Mignola*
*978-1-59582-501-8 • $17.99*

**THE DARK HORSE BOOK OF HORROR**
*Story and art by Mike Mignola and various*
*978-1-50672-864-3 • $24.99*

**THE SHAOLIN COWBOY: SHEMP BUFFET**
*Story and art by Geof Darrow*
*978-1-61655-726-3 • $19.99*

**BEASTS OF BURDEN: ANIMAL RITES**
*Story by Evan Dorkin*
*Art by Jill Thompson*
*978-1-59582-513-1 • $19.99*

**EDGAR ALLAN POE'S SPIRITS OF THE DEAD**
*Story and art by Richard Corben*
*978-1-61655-356-2 • $24.99*

**RAT GOD**
*Story and art by Richard Corben*
*978-1-61655-769-0 • $19.99*

**HARROW COUNTY VOLUME 1: COUNTLESS HAINTS**
*Story by Cullen Bunn*
*Art by Tyler Crook*
*978-1-61655-780-5 • $14.99*

**ALEISTER & ADOLF**
*Story by Douglas Rushkoff*
*Art by Michael Avon Oeming*
*978-1-50670-104-2 • $19.99*

**GARY GIANNI'S MONSTERMEN AND OTHER SCARY STORIES**
*Story and art by Gary Gianni*
*978-1-50670-480-7 • $19.99*

**THE SHADOW GLASS**
*Story and art by Aly Fell*
*978-1-50670-082-3 • $19.99*

**BERNIE WRIGHTSON'S FRANKENSTEIN**
*Story by Mary Wollstonecraft Shelley*
*Art by Bernie Wrightson*
*978-1-59582-200-0 • $34.99*

**DEAR CREATURE**
*Story and art by Jonathan Case*
*978-1-50670-095-3 • $22.99*

**BEDTIME GAMES**
*Story by Nick Keller*
*Art by Conor Nolan*
*978-1-50670-901-7 • $17.99*

**JENNY FINN**
*Story by Mike Mignola and Troy Nixey*
*Art by Troy Nixey and Farel Dalrymple*
*978-1-50670-544-6 • $17.99*

**SHADOWS ON THE GRAVE**
*Story and art by Richard Corben*
*978-1-50670-391-6 • $19.99*

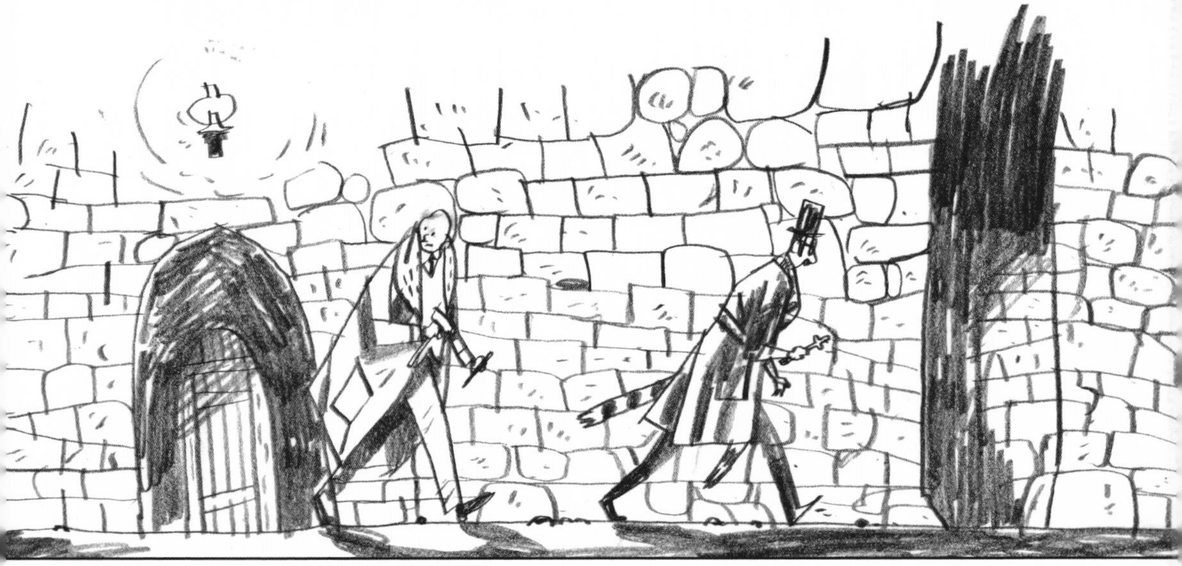